# Kessen's Kronikles

## The Adventures of a Cross Country Canine

**by**
**Jennifer Rae**

*Jennifer Rae*

i

# Copyright Notices

**Jennifer Rae Trojan Publishing**

kessenskronikles@gmail.com

### International Standard Book Number
### (ISBN) 0-9766965-2-5

# Disclaimer

This is a work of fiction. Names, characters, places, events and incidents are either the products of the author's imagination or used in a fictitious manner.

# Cover Photos

©2012 Courtesy of Lisa Kruss | petphotos.com

# DEDICATION

To my adoptive mom and dad who gave me:

Unconditional love even when I didn't deserve it...

Standards of appropriate behavior even though

I thought them to be silly...

And above all,

Eventually allowed me to sleep on the couch.

# THE INVITATION

To say this is just another story about a cute, adventurous and somewhat mischievous dog would short change the dog. I know this for a fact since *I am that dog* and can tell you that while I am definitely cute...some might even say handsome...my story goes beyond appearances as well as the typical story of a dog's life. It is a roller coaster ride filled with adventures, hopes and dreams. I cordially invite you to ride along...no ticket necessary...no height requirement to ride. Just sit back and enjoy as the adventures begin.

*From the moment she held me in her arms on that bitter, cold, winter night, I knew I was safe, but my life would never be the same...*

**Kessen**

# Kessen's Kronikles

# PART I
## THE ACCIDENT

When I was four years old, my mom and dad thought it would be fun to drive across the country from our western suburb of Chicago, Illinois to California and back.

*California…here we come!*

We would travel via the historical Route 66, also known as the Main Street of America. Since my adopted sister Brightie was visiting friends for a few weeks, the three of us took to the highway in our trusty Volvo station wagon that my mom lovingly named Sparky 2. It was our second Volvo, and she thought of it as her Sparkler on Wheels. Seriously? A sparkler on wheels? It was a station wagon!

Anyway, we began our adventure to the Golden State with great enthusiasm. However, my mom wasn't the best car traveler and decided to amuse herself by learning to play the harmonica. *She* was amused; I'll leave it at that. All the same, it did make the time pass as the roads and scenery

3

changed from state to state. Mountains changed in color from brown to fiery red. Grass was no longer green, but took on the hues of sun bleached browns and became desert like in texture. Rest stop areas for dogs were no longer soft on the pads of my paws but prickly from what I later learned was something called tumbleweed. Because I possess a relatively large bladder, I didn't have to make too many stops and was grateful for that organ's capacity. I just knew the size of my bladder would come in handy some day and was thankful for my genetic makeup.

Nevertheless, the car was filled with harmonic sounds that at times stunned the senses as the winding roads took us closer to California. By the time we reached our destination, my mom could play a mean version of the *Battle Hymn of the Republic.* At night, her attempts to lull us into dreamland with her version of *Taps* were, in themselves, sleep inducing. Perhaps it was a form of survival mode for my dad and me. We didn't question it, but went willingly to sleep to avoid an encore.

I had been a pretty good dog on the way to California and had been relegated to the back seat of the car for the entire trip. Although the back seat was comfortable, I thought a seating change might be in order for the return trip home. Somewhere along the stretch of Route 66 in New

Mexico, ideas began to fill my mind. The perfect plan was taking shape, and "Operation Front Seat" was formed. I was going to have some fun by *messing with the parents*. My goal was to be granted a position in the front seat with the grownups. In my mind, it was mischief with a purpose.

After all, I believed that I deserved to be in the front seat of the car. While I'm not proud of my intent or my methods, I had to do something to relieve the boredom of being a back seat passenger. Preventing my mother from breaking out that harmonica again was secondary to my original plan, but it was unquestionably, a relevant part of the plan's outcome.

So "Operation Front Seat" began. My first move was to put my head lovingly on my dad's shoulder while he was driving.

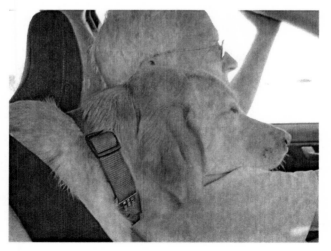

*Quite the slick move on my part.*

The tactic was different, but not so bold as to call attention to my goal of reaching the front seat. Adding a tender gaze and a sigh of contentment, I knew that I had them hooked. I heard the *oohs* and *ahhs* of what a good dog I was and the click of the camera etching my face into the history of the trip. Not a hint of devious intent was thought to exist; I knew I had them in the pads of my paws.

The time to move toward the front seat was *now or never* as the words "go for it" bounced around my mind. My parents had been so receptive to my big, brown eyes and soulful look that I was convinced this was my big moment. My plan was working, or so I thought. My hackles were tingling with excitement as I began my forward lunge ever so gently toward the front seat. Pride in my ingenuity filled my senses and gave me the courage to add momentum to my forward lunge. How could such a good plan not work?

Let me tell you...The explosive sound of the word "NO" stopped me before my hind legs left the back seat. It resonated through my skull as though it were delivered through an air horn. My first thoughts were that I might never hear properly again or may have suffered mild brain damage. While momentarily startled, I was able to gradually shake it off, regroup and pull it together. I was now more determined than ever to follow through with my plan.

6

Given the situation, the prospect of having potential hearing loss and mild brain interruption was momentarily discouraging. On the other paw, I had the delusional thought that perhaps they were joking with me just to avoid the boredom of the endless miles. After all, they did have a sense of humor. I tried again, and this time the results were very different.

At the speed of light, they pulled off the road and shifted the luggage in the car. With the deftness of a magician's hand, they had me incarcerated in my canvas crate. The Penalty Box was now occupied by me. I was surrounded by luggage and viewing the New Mexico skyline through canvas netting. My decision making skills were not up to par on that day, and freedom was forfeited for messing with the folks. The plan had definitely gone wrong, and "Operation Front Seat" was a failure.

As the skyline drifted past and the scenery changed from grass to bushes to tumbleweed, I was lulled into a partial dozing state by the sound of the car's wheels bouncing atop the heated pavement. Little did I know that my world was about to change, and it was not for the better.

Suddenly, I was startled by my mother's shrill cry of "Watch Out!" My dad was driving around 80 miles an hour in the far lane of the road. He said nothing, but gripped the steering wheel with an intensity that I had never witnessed. In front of us was something resembling a huge log bouncing erratically across the highway. With no set pattern to the object's directions, my dad was finding it difficult to avoid it. Sadly, his attempts failed.

The hurling object was the drive shaft from an incapacitated semi-trailer truck ahead of us. It bounced under our trusty Sparky 2's chassis causing a grinding, chain saw-like sound that reverberated from the car's underside as it worked its way toward freedom. The screeching sound of metal grinding as it ripped the underside of the car to bits seemed to last forever as the car shuddered and bucked to the side of the road.

My Penalty Box became my security while I was tossed and tumbled around the car's back seat. Then, amidst the acrid smell of smoke, burning rubber, shattering glass and the sound of the engine gently dying, I began seeing events of my life. At first, they were in strobe like flashes, but surprisingly were appearing in chronological order. Was I hallucinating? Perhaps I was, but my life experiences and events didn't stop.

Following the accident, the light around me began to fade. No motion from the front seat of the car could be seen and sounds were becoming faint echoes. I found myself clinging to my life yet staring at my beginnings. Was seeing my life flash before me meant to serve as consolation for the loss that was about to occur? An eerie hush began to take over my senses. As blackness began to engulf me, my last thoughts were of that wonderful meadow with the bluest of blue skies where it all began...

# PART II
# LIVING THE GOOD LIFE

*My name is Kessen.*

# 1

## The Early Days

The California sun is shining so brightly that even the clouds don't dare show their faces against the bluest of blue skies. I can honestly say that because I've been watching the sky all day while rolling around on my back and periodically munching on blades of grass. It's such a peaceful and seemingly safe existence in this meadow of mine.

Where are my manners? Please allow me to introduce myself...my name is Kessen. I am six weeks old, live with my birth mother, two adult caretakers and six other siblings in a city not far from San Francisco, California. I'm told that I am part Golden Retriever and part Labrador Retriever, but I can't tell you which part is which. When I gaze into the nearby pond, I see my reflection, and I must admit that I am quite the looker. Mind you, I'm not being boastful; I'm just being honest. My fluffy, short, golden coat surrounds a mass of wrinkles covering my face in contrast to the coal, black nose that seems to draw attention to my expressive eyes. I'm told that I will eventually grow into my wrinkles...if that's even possible. My nose might even turn from black to pink. As if

13

that isn't enough, I was also born with a black dot of fur on my right side near my ribs. My sister Kelyn nicknamed it my "doorbell" and likes to poke it now and then. She thinks that she's a comedian, but I'll talk a bit more about her later.

Now, I think I can handle the wrinkle issue, but I can't do anything about the "doorbell" on my side. I also believe that I am suave enough to carry off a pink nose with dignity. However, I am fearful of what they say about my paws. They've been equated to the size of hamburger patties. What does that even mean? It certainly can't be good since it refers to something edible. I'm going to seek some advice about that from the older puppies in the household.

*What's happening with my paws?*

I also think of myself as being a bit of a contradiction since I consider myself to be both cool and not so cool at the same time. What makes me cool is the tattoo in my ear, but the not so cool part is that it's nothing wild and crazy. There's no serpent wrapped around an anchor or a pirate's face staring out at the world through my ear. It's nothing that declares me manly. Instead, it's just a number signifying my birth date. It's like a person's social security number, but housed in my ear instead of on a card in a wallet. As mundane as my tattoo is, I learned later in life that just having a tattoo is quite the magnet for cute canines!

Those are my official credentials, but I can tell you right now that I am more than just a combination of genes. I am told that I am a puppy who is destined for service as an assistance dog. Do I even know what that means? I can tell you with the utmost certainty that I don't have a clue. I'm just a free spirit running amuck all day long with my other siblings.

Let's talk about them for a moment. They are quite the rowdy bunch which is why I spend a lot of time by myself or with Kelyn. She is not only my sister but also my very best friend. She is so beautiful, and I wish I could say ladylike, but she'd grab the scruff of my neck and shake me with a great deal of force if she heard me say that about her. She's one tough pup. Kelyn can race rings around our other siblings, gulp her meals faster than the speed of light, belch louder than any of us and catch a bug in midair. She's the greatest!

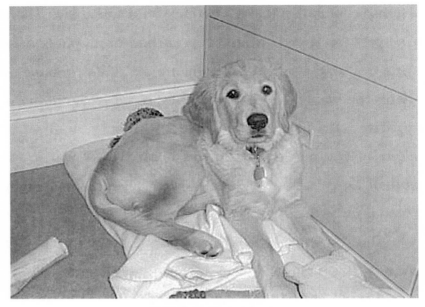

*Kelyn is pretty, but tough.*

She is also very quick to point out my shortcomings: monster paws, short coat when all of the other litter mates have long, flowing coats and that nose of mine that might turn pink. She also tells me that I have a few character flaws and a tendency to be boastful. I can't help that I was born with the ability to communicate, at times, in both the canine and the human world. I consider myself to be bilingual, and it's my obligation to use this ability for the greater good. It's a gift and not any colossal accomplishment. I'm just telling it like it is!

*Honesty is the best policy.*

Kelyn also thinks that I am, at times, somewhat arrogant. Of course, she is right. Who else but my best friend would be so honest with me? In spite of my flaws, we just enjoy being with each other. Spending time with her, air snapping, jaw sparring, chewing on grass and occasionally throwing up is such great fun. If this is what life is all about, then I'm in it for the long haul. These early days make one's life worth living.

Nevertheless, I was soon to learn that nothing stays the same; and my once cloudless, blue sky will be shaded with ominous warnings of things to come. A few weeks later, my idyllic world would be changed drastically, and it will all start with something as simple as a car ride...

17

## 2

# The Car Ride

The day began like any other day. I was now eight weeks old, had been eating regular puppy food for a few weeks, was growing into my wrinkles and just enjoying myself. I passed the time by chasing butterflies, munching on grass or jaw sparring with Kelyn. Mostly, I liked rolling around in the meadow, taking time to watch the blue sky, dreaming about adventures and actually seeing a cloud once in a while.

My birth mother didn't spend too much time with us anymore since we were eating regular puppy food, but she was always there to correct us when foolish behavior took precedence over common sense. She guided us through the difficult times with her gentle nudging or, if necessary, a more direct method of persuasion...the dreaded neck scruff shake. (*I dare you to say that five times fast.*) Anyway, the close bond we had with her seemed a bit different as we became more independent. Yet, we always knew she'd be there for us, so we continued to behave foolishly whenever we had the chance. After all, we were young and enjoying the good life.

19

Today seemed different, and I'm not sure why I felt that way. Perhaps the funny feeling in my stomach was due to the sight of darkened clouds in the sky. Kelyn thought it might be gas from the beans they put in our morning meal or perhaps a thunder storm approaching. It was more than that. This was a feeling that I had never experienced before and surrounding that feeling was a sense of fear.

The first and only time I ever felt that way was when the neighbor's dog, who we called Big Bully Dog, had managed to find an opening in the fence and used that to his advantage in terms of surprising us. We were all yapping and barking as he chased us around the yard. Even though we were scared, we had the advantage since there were seven of us. He never quite knew who to focus on in his attempt to frighten us. With his eyes crossed from trying to catch all of us and his labored breathing from the chase, I do believe we confused him into exhaustion. Tongue hanging almost to the ground, he finally gave up, went back to his opening in the fence and eventually dragged himself back to his own dog house. We were lucky. Had he been a herding dog, we would have been in big trouble. That was my first and only experience with fear, but this sensation of mine was more than fear. Something was going to happen, and it wasn't going to be good. I could feel it.

My brothers and sisters went about their day...playing, running, laughing about the big dog next door and his crazed look while trying to focus his eyes as he chased us. They had forgotten how frightened we all were when it was happening. I didn't forget and just couldn't join in their fun. I still had this terrible feeling that something bad was going to happen. Why couldn't I find a way to shake it off?

Seeing the car pull into our driveway sent a chill through my body and caused the hackles on my neck to tingle. I could not figure out why I was having such a reaction since we had cars pull into our driveway before. Somehow, this was different. In the past, we had gone on car rides, and those were fun. We usually visited other puppies' homes, had special treats, played in the grass and got lots of attention from children and adults. We even went to San Francisco once for puppy checkups, saw the big ships in the wharf, listened to the harbor seals and heard the airplanes coming and going as we passed the airport. Those trips were special, yet something about this car ride was very different.

I didn't know how it was different until I saw that there were no towels, water bottles, bowls or toys being placed in the car. Only travel crates filled the back portion of the car...those hard ones having holes in the sides and metal, checkerboard-like doors. This was not a good sign and definitely was not a typical car ride.

I looked over and saw my birth mother staring at us from a distance. Before this moment, I had never seen such sadness in her eyes. Even though we had been pretty much on our own for the last week or so, we still had so much more to learn from her. We needed her and believed that she would always be there for us. What was happening?

However, what we needed or wanted really didn't matter. Our adult caretakers, looking a bit sad as well, began loading us into the crates. I was lucky to be put with Kelyn who was beside herself with fear and confusion. She was always the strong, brave one, and now, as she moved closer and closer to me, I could see she was terrified. I realized that I had to be strong for her, and I didn't have a clue as to where to start. Bravery was never one of my strengths.

As the car started down the driveway, I could still see my birth mother through the metal door of the crate. Her image was getting smaller and smaller as the car made its way to the road. I tried to memorize every bit of her face and her loving eyes. Thoughts of the warmth of her body at night when we snuggled next to her and how her soft, flowing coat glistened in the sunlight echoed in my brain. Not knowing what to do, yet realizing that I only had one opportunity to give her some sort of sign of my love and appreciation for everything she had done for us, I put my paw on the crate's door as if to wave good bye to her. I'd like to think she saw me and understood, but I can't be sure. We were now on our way to someplace unknown to us, and I will readily admit that we were all very worried...

# 3

## The Reluctant Traveler

Confusion gave way to exhaustion as the car drove
through the California countryside. Vineyards flanked the
highway as we continued to some unknown destination, and
my mind was consumed with loss. Would I ever see my birth
mother again, run in the meadow, chase butterflies or just feel
safe one more time? I wasn't sure of anything. I just knew
that my world changed, and it wasn't for the better.

Kelyn was asleep for most of the trip; and within a few
hours, our car turned into a beautiful, tree lined driveway. It
came to a stop within a few feet of a building that looked
quite inviting with its dog caricatures lining the sidewalks
and barking dogs welcoming us from behind the walls. As
nice as it seemed, it wasn't home. So I wasn't having
anything to do with it.

We were carefully unloaded from the crates and put in
a play yard equipped with all sorts of toys, other puppies and
smiling adults who were welcoming us to this new place.
Our adult caretakers, not smiling like the others, gave us each
loving hugs and left us alone in this strange, new place. As I

25

have said before, nothing stays the same, and it was all just too confusing.

After a while, we were taken one by one and placed in yet another set of crates. This time, our mode of transportation was a van. It was different from the car in that it was very large and the crates had the words *Airline Carrier* on their sides. This was not a good sign. What was worse was that Kelyn was nowhere to be found. The last I saw of her was in the play yard showing off her ability to catch a bug in midair. I was supposed to take care of her. Instead, I'm being loaded into an airline carrier with a strange puppy who is not even one of my siblings. He also doesn't seem to want a roommate. I could tell that by his body language. Baring his teeth, curling his lip and uttering a raspy, guttural growl were fairly large clues. I'm very perceptive when it comes to things like that. I kept my distance, put off the introduction and attempted to stay out of his way.

I tried not to let the feelings of frustration overwhelm me. Not only was I sequestered in a carrier with an unfriendly puppy, I was also on some sort of trip to who knew where. Thoughts jumbled around my brain. I might never see Kelyn again, and I never even got to say good bye to her. There were just too many losses in one day. I wanted to give in to exhaustion but had to keep one eye open in case my less than friendly roomy decided to pounce on me while I was asleep. I am a thinker…not a fighter. While totally inept at physical altercations, I avoid them at all costs, and I willed myself to stay awake.

Well, as if moving about in cars and vans weren't enough, the words *Airline Carrier* would soon take on real meaning. Passing over the Golden Gate Bridge into the city of San Francisco and traveling along the Embarcadero might have been a great car ride if the circumstances had been different. I was pretty sure we had traveled this route on our trip for our puppy checkups a few weeks earlier, so maybe this wasn't as bad as I feared. Seeing the huge ships lingering along the wharf, with the sounds of the harbor seals echoing in the background, confirmed my suspicions that we were nearing the airport and more unknowns. Within minutes, I could hear the roar of airplanes overhead. The noise from their take offs and landings overshadowed the noise of taxicab horns as their drivers jockeyed for spaces next to the curbs. I was so utterly bewildered by the combination of sights and sounds.

Our van made its way to a special parking area; and before long, we were passengers on an airplane. Early this morning, I was chomping on grass in the California sunshine; and within hours, I was closeted in an airline carrier with a

27

disgruntled roommate. Life sure turned on a dime; and in this economy, a dime sure wasn't worth much.

After a few hours in the air, we reached our destination and, might I add, kudos to the pilot for a most comfortable landing. Our carrier was loaded onto yet another vehicle. Sorry to say, I was getting used to the various modes of transportation. This time, it was a fork lift that took us into a cargo location. Did the fork lift surprise me? Strangely, it did not. At this point, they could bring in a covered wagon, and it wouldn't bother me one bit. I had been in or on more types of transportation in one day than in my entire life. I just didn't care anymore.

Since I am able to read, which is part of my being bilingual, I saw the sign that read..."Welcome to Chicago." Chicago? What or where is a Chicago? I was just about ready to give a howl that would rock this carrier, when my disgruntled roomy, Mister Not So Nice, belted out a screech that sent my eyes revolving around my head. The beast not only speaks...he screeches! The first sound out of his mouth since his less than friendly welcome to me a few hours ago is a gut wrenching, ear shattering sound. Yikes! It even brought my resting hackles to attention. The adults waiting for us seemed to show great concern over the blast of noise coming from our carrier.

"I hope that's not *my* puppy!" was heard from outside the carrier. Well, I wasn't going to take the blame for that outburst. I just sat nicely in the carrier and demonstrated the manners that my birth mother taught me. Gosh, I missed her and I missed everything about my life. I doubted that I would ever feel safe again.

*That noise did **not** come from me.*

As the carrier door opened, a pleasant looking couple walked towards us, and the woman gently lifted me from the carrier. She was careful not to jostle or frighten me any more than I already was. The man, who was quite handsome, rubbed my paws and my back. As the woman held me up to her face, I saw kindness in her eyes. She added, "Welcome to your new family."

*What?* Those words startled me from my temporary sense of relief. I had been in a car, a van, an airplane and on a fork lift today. I'm not really caring about any new family right now. Having kind eyes and gentle hands just wasn't going to cut it. I want my own family, and I want them now! I know that sounds harsh, especially after being shown such kindness, but I had reached the end of my leash. For the record, I had never even been on a leash, so you know I was way out there in terms of emotions. There's only so much a puppy can take!

Once again, it wasn't what I wanted or needed that mattered. I was whisked away by these two new adults. They attached a cotton lead to my puppy collar and placed me on the ground to get the traveling kinks out of my legs.

*What is this stuff?*

Taken entirely by surprise, I found myself surrounded by a mass of white, mushy, cold stuff called snow. Within seconds, I do believe the pads of my paws were starting to go numb from this stuff; and the bitter, cold wind was closing my nasal passages…possibly freezing my face. Add insult to injury, all of the day's emotional upsets, coupled with not eating, brought on a condition that we pups called "the squirts." Believe me, it is not pretty, and willing it to stop is ineffective. The intestinal tract has a mind of its own; elimination, in this form, is its own version of revenge.

Could this day get any worse? Now, what am I going to do? Please let this entire day be a terrible nightmare brought on by eating too much grass in the meadow. That would account for the "squirts." I had been warned about that consequence many times but never heeded the warnings. My decision making skills were definitely lacking, and this was not the first time I was attacked by my intestinal tract. Regrettably, this wasn't a dream. It was real and was my unsolicited introduction not only to a new place to live, but to a Midwest winter.

After a few minutes, another car pulled up in front of us. Don't people ever run out of modes of transportation? I guess not, but at least it wasn't a covered wagon. I was told that we were all going to my new home. *They're taking me to a new home?* I already have a home, and it isn't in this cold, snow-filled, awful place. While I might have to go along with this for now, I simply refuse to call it home. Another news flash...I wasn't going to cooperate in any way, shape or form since I was a reluctant traveler.

I was sad, frustrated, scared, cold and now, thanks to the revolt in my intestinal tract, pretty messy. My body shook from the cold, from the fear that overwhelmed me and from loss of dignity. I just wanted to go home...to *my* home. As the chills continued, the woman with the kind eyes used a warm cloth to sanitize my butt and wrapped me in a soft, sweet smelling blanket for warmth. Perhaps she was just protecting herself from the next attack of the "squirts." Who knew at this point? She continued to hold me on her lap and kept saying nice things to me. She talked about how lucky she and her husband were to have me, what a good puppy I was and how she didn't know that she could love a puppy so much...so soon. As she held me closer, I could feel her heart beating, and it made me miss my birth mother all the more.

Then, a strange thing happened. A sudden sense of relief and calmness seemed to wash over me. Maybe it was the sheer exhaustion of the day that caused me to go limp in her arms. All of the traveling, the confusion and the terrible losses of today seemed faint echoes in my mind; I didn't understand this feeling. From the moment she held me in her arms on that bitter, cold, winter night, I knew I was safe, but my life would never be the same...

# 4

# Letting Go

I'm three months old now and have been the *puppy in residence* for four weeks. I refuse to call it home, so I refer to it merely as my place of residence. Snow continues to fall, day after day; and it is still cold, wet and mushy. The gentle husband makes sure that he shovels some space for me in a dog run before I am sent outside. Still, I refuse to be grateful, and that's a side of me that I hardly recognize. I cling to the memories of my California home, but lately, those memories seem to be fading. I can no longer see my birth mother's face clearly, can't picture Kelyn's antics and don't think about my other siblings. Even the cloudless, blue sky covering my meadow is growing dim in my mind. There's no blue sky here...just gray skies, snow and blustery winds. With each passing day, memories and images of my home are becoming faint echoes in my mind. That frightens me. Without those recollections, what will I have left?

I wasn't the best of pups when I first arrived here about four weeks ago. The last stop on my Reluctant Traveler Express was this house in a western suburb of Chicago, Illinois. It was already night time when we finally arrived, and I had been traveling since early morning. The woman with the kind eyes had me go outside once again into the snow and then gave me a warm meal of chicken and rice to help settle my intestinal turmoil. Afterwards, she lured me into yet another type of carrier called a kennel. It was made of wire, had a soft, warm bed and a cuddly toy positioned in the corner. Unlike the airline carrier, I was able to look out from all sides. While a room with a view might have its appeal, it held nothing of importance for this reluctant traveler. As far as I was concerned, this open concept kennel was just another form of incarceration.

Shamefully, I demonstrated my lack of gratitude in the only way I felt fitting. I howled endlessly that first night taking only brief moments for gulps of air and for a few minutes of sleep before resuming my performances. I continued that process periodically for days. The woman with the kind eyes and her handsome husband just seemed to tolerate my behavior. They never raised their voices or expressed concern that I might be experiencing some form of respiratory distress because of my constant wailing. During an intermission of one of my arias, I did hear the woman say that perhaps I wasn't meant to be an assistance dog; perhaps being an opera singer was my path in life. My choices were either an assistance dog or an opera singer? Was she offering career counseling, or was it an attempt at sarcasm? I wasn't sure, but I was determined to find a way for them to send me back to my home.

When I was in my kennel, I howled off and on...day after day...night after night for about two weeks. This kind couple either ignored me or covered the kennel with a sheet. Then, I was struck with an odd thought...perhaps they were deaf, and all of my howling efforts were in vain. I was wrong about that as well. They continued to overlook my behavior and often left the room when I really got carried away with tossing toys, pulling on their clothes with my razor sharp teeth or just being rude. Leaving me alone was worse than yelling at me, yet they didn't give in to my antics. Apparently, my plans lacked thought and substance. After all, I was still there.

Worse than their kindness was the fact that in spite of my belligerent behavior, the kind woman would scoop me up every night, hold me gently even though I struggled and would sing to me. She alternated between the first verses of *You Are My Sunshine* and *Let Me Call You Sweetheart*.

I was a brat day in and day out, yet she continued to sing to me every night. She told me that no matter how much I'd resist and no matter how long it would take, she would continue to do this singing ritual for the entire time I was to spend in their house. The ritual was meant to provide a calming influence and help me sleep through the night.

My thought process quickly delved into possible alternatives. Should I give in and possibly have her stop singing, or should I continue to resist? Maybe she'd give up, discontinue the ritual or at least change the songs. I did have strategic choices, but which one would insure the best outcome? Since I couldn't decide which one would be the most productive, I just continued to struggle.

Now to be honest, it wasn't all that bad. Had I been in a different frame of mind, I might have felt reassured by her soothing voice; but I just couldn't give up the struggle. If I did that, it would mean that I had given up on the prospect of ever going back to my home. I wasn't ready to do that.

Consequently, I had my own ritual. She'd scoop me up into her arms. I'd struggle until she finished the song, and she'd put me in my kennel. Then, I'd howl for a while and eventually fall asleep. It was as simple as that.

*My ritual was simple, but exhausting.*

Deep down, I was not proud of my behavior, but I couldn't stop...not while there was still hope of ever going home.

One can't rely on hope alone. As my homeward bound plans fell apart one by one, I began to see the futility of my efforts. I had to find a way to make this work for me. Maybe if I got them to trust me, I could one day escape. That was one of my sillier thoughts. How would I get all of those various modes of transportation together to get me back home? It just wasn't a workable plan. Mind you, I wasn't giving up; I was just waiting for inspiration.

*There has to be a way to get back home.*

The real breakthrough came for me on a day like no other day. I call it my day of reckoning. I was now allowed to run freely in the fenced yard and was having such fun making serpentine paths through the bushes. In my peripheral vision, I happened to spot another dog on the other side of the fence. He was a beautiful Golden Retriever with a long, flowing coat and such a regal face. As he ambled over to the fence line, I rushed with great speed to meet him. The thought of making a new friend was so overwhelming that my depth perception was a bit off...to say the least. Because my enthusiasm and excessive speed exceeded my spatial perception, I found that while my head fit through the space between the fence rails, somehow, the reverse didn't work. Now, my head was stuck, and my opportunity for a good, first impression was missed. I tried to look cool and unperturbed at my predicament, but that façade faded very quickly. I began to flail around hoping my head would just either get a bit smaller from my actions or that the space between the fence rails would somehow miraculously expand from my phenomenal strength. I had no such luck.

The regal looking neighbor dog, knowing that he couldn't help, looked at me with a slight grin and said, "I'll catch you later when your head's on straight." With that, he turned and went back to his house.

Great. Not only did I look foolish, but I was living next to a comedian. I wasn't sure what to do since flailing around didn't solve the problem; so I did what I did best. I screeched like I never screeched before. It was the screech heard 'round the world! While I do tend to exaggerate, it probably was only heard 'round the neighborhood or more realistically within the block. Needless to say, it was a cry for help and what did I hear myself yelling? "Help me, Mom...please help me!"

I was now calling the kind eyed woman my mom. I must have incurred a head injury from the fence debacle and was delirious. She came running from the other side of the yard at the sound of my screeching and saw what had happened. As she knelt down beside me, she talked in a soothing voice while rubbing my back and head. I could feel myself relaxing. When my body went totally limp, she moved my head a little to the left and then to the right. My head was once again free of the fence rails. She calmly said, "You're fine now...such a brave pup...you can go and play."

She didn't coo, cuddle or remind me about the relationship between head size and width of space between fence rails. There was no lecture, but not one bit of sympathy for my plight either. She just told me that I was fine and had been a very brave puppy. That's it? I had what I believed to be a near death experience and was not given one bit of sympathy for my predicament. It was unbelievable!

Once past those dramatic thoughts, I was reminded that in my time of need I had called her Mom. As I sat in the middle of the yard, far from the dreaded fence line, my thought process kicked in, and I had to ask myself why I called her that. Well...she fed me, made sure I had a warm place to sleep, sang to me and tolerated my foolish behavior. She also kept me safe. That's what moms do; and if I hadn't been so stubborn, I would have realized that she had already become my new mom because of all of the things she had done and was doing for me every day. Perhaps, I'm not as smart as I thought; that possibility was a real blow to my ego.

It seemed that I had already accepted the fact that my past was just that...a closed chapter in my life. This was my opportunity to move forward toward the future and begin a new chapter in my life. In order to make that work for me, I had to let go of the plans to ever return to my home in California...really let go, not just in my mind, but in my heart as well. What I also realized with a jolt was that I had been doing just that these past few weeks.

I decided to take a risk on perhaps finding happiness again, and it would start with my calling the woman with the kind eyes by her new name...Mom. The handsome, gentle man, who always had a kind word for me and slipped me treats when no one was looking, would now be called Dad. I would make them my new family; and even though they wouldn't be the same as my California family, it was my choice to be happy once again. This was a huge leap of faith for me, but I did pride myself in being a risk taker. It suddenly felt like a huge weight was lifted from my shoulders...I was finally home.

*This feels right.*

I learned a few lessons on that particular day. While I felt brave and confident following the fence incident, I never went close to the fence line again. Lesson Number One was learned, and I wasn't going to tempt fate. Lesson Number Two dealt with letting go; and while it was definitely not easy, it was the only way to move forward towards enjoyment in life. Doesn't sound like me, does it? What I considered to be a near death experience must have brought out the philosopher in me. I went from fool to philosopher in the span of an afternoon.

Nevertheless, it was how I felt on that particular day and at that particular moment in time. My euphoria was short lived when I heard my mom (*I liked the sound of that.*) tell me that I had to get a good night's sleep because tomorrow was a big day. I was starting school. School? I didn't even know what that was, yet I sensed excitement from the tone of her voice. The thought of having a fun filled adventure was surely promising, but a hint of apprehension crept along the sidelines of my brain. Based upon past experiences, I was somewhat suspicious of what tomorrow would bring...

# 5

## School Days

This was a day that promised fun and adventure. I was going to school for the very first time and had a restless night due to my anticipation of the coming events. Since some of my breakfast was going to be used for treats while in class, my morning meal was a bit Spartan, but I didn't care. My excitement was building, and I just couldn't wait to get there. While I didn't know where I was going, I just knew it was going to be special. My mom had brushed my soft, golden coat, checked my eyes, ears and paws as she did every day, but also prepared a traveling bag that held updated vaccination papers, a water bottle, bowl, paper towels, collars and poop bags. I was ready to rock and roll.

Because I had some time before we were to leave, I went into my kennel to rest. I often did that without being told. It had become my open concept home within the family home...a thinker's paradise. While waiting, my mind wandered to thoughts of the past few weeks and some of the things that had happened to me once I decided to cooperate with the family.

In between my earlier rants and raves, I spent some time each day adjusting to new experiences. I was introduced to two different types of collars. One was a flat collar that went around my neck, and the other was a head collar. Getting used to the head collar was tricky since it had a strip of material that looped around my muzzle. That strip reminded me of my birth mother's method of correction. She would re-direct my actions, foolish or otherwise, by putting her mouth on my muzzle. Remembering that was a bit comforting, but I still wasn't ready to give in to the loss of control. Anyway, my mom would put it on me, take it off and give me a treat. She would do this over and over again during the day until one day I just didn't mind wearing it. After all, I was getting treats...even if they were parts of my breakfast, lunch and dinner set aside as rewards for my good behavior. This treat situation fooled me at first, but I eventually caught on to what was happening. The learning process is so humbling.

Another form of restraint was introduced: the dreaded leash. This adjustment took some time since most of my endeavors found me stretching by my neck trying to get somewhere that was ultimately out of my reach. I eventually compromised on that as well, but not without a fight and not without periodic lapses in proper leash behavior. My resolve was dwindling back then and I didn't even know it was happening.

I was also learning to follow words called commands. Mind you, they weren't tricks; they were considered rules of behavior. It was all part of my preparation for being a potential assistance dog as well as being a respectful pet...I called it Great Expectations! My mom told me that if I worked very hard, followed directions and learned all of my commands, I might someday be a helper dog to someone in need. To be honest, I wasn't very impressed with that potential. I was just interested in the treats. Had I always been so shallow?

What I discovered was that when I did things they wanted me to, I'd get a treat and lots of praise. If I didn't do what was asked, I'd get nothing. The realization that I did, indeed, have some control in my life was totally awesome. I was taking back my individuality, and I didn't even know it was happening. I felt such a surge of confidence with that new found power and displayed a bit of strut to my step when I walked...even on the dreaded leash. I could pick and choose what I wanted to do. POWER TO THE PUP became my mantra. I was ready for anything...not only on that day, but every day as well.

My thoughts of the past learning experiences were interrupted with my being called from my kennel and placed in the car's canvas crate. I still had bad memories of mobile travel, so I simply refused to look out the windows. There just might be a fork lift around the corner. I just lay quietly in the crate and hugged my cuddly toy for comfort. I kept repeating my mantra, POWER TO THE PUP, for support and courage. I could do this...it was just school, and I had to believe it was going to be fun. After all, my mom packed the treat pouch!

We reached a huge building; and when I was taken out of the car, I heard a lot of barking coming from the building. Suddenly, I wasn't frightened anymore...instead, I was excited. The barking sounded friendly, and I could really use a canine friend about now. My new family was great, but they weren't puppies. As we went inside, I have to admit that everything I had learned about walking on a leash went by the wayside. I stretched and stretched on that leash just to get where the action was.

Someone from beyond the entrance door was welcoming the pups to Puppy Kindergarten. There were puppies of all sizes in the class. I was one of the tallest breeds, but definitely not the loudest since I learned weeks earlier that

50

there were no positive gains from barking or howling. In my opinion, noises like that were exercises in futility.

My dad and I were going to work as a team, and that was going to be fun.

*This was going to be fun.*

There were also quite a few pups in the new class. There was a Miniature Poodle who didn't make eye contact with any of us and an English Sheepdog who looked at me as if to say, "Bring it on, Dude." (*Does anyone talk like that anymore, let alone a puppy?*) Then, there was the Brittany Spaniel, who was only concerned with field work and why we weren't working in a field. This was Puppy Kindergarten...not the forest preserve! There were other pups...the timid Beagle, the howling Bassett Hound and the perky, chocolate colored Labrador Retriever.

Then, there was Tom. I recognized a kindred spirit when I saw one. He and I made eye contact, and we both knew this was going to be a fun class. He was a very unique and expensive breed whose name I couldn't pronounce...let alone spell, but Tom wasn't full of himself because of his breed's status. He was just Tom, and what you saw was what you got. The mischievous gleam in his eyes led me to believe that we were going to be the best of friends. I just knew it.

So class began with the basics...introductions, learning to recognize our names, how to maintain eye contact and how to sit properly. I already knew those things so I could do them while observing the other pups. The Poodle was stubborn, the English Sheepdog couldn't be bothered and the Brittany was still hopeful for a Field of Dreams to somehow appear within the concrete walls of the training facility. Tom and I just followed directions while making faces at each other from across the room. The other pups were all over the place...especially the Labrador Retriever. In addition to being perky, he was quite the ball of energy. He was getting up and down from his SITs while barking enthusiastically in his quest for treats. There was never a dull moment in this class. I never knew controlled chaos could be such fun.

Now, let's talk about our own version of Field of Dreams. Puppy Kindergarten was not only a place for learning but also a place for play time called Socialization Time. The Brittany was going to get her wish, but not in the form she wanted. We were all let loose to run and play. Oh, we had such fun. Tom and I chased each other while the others followed our lead. The English Sheepdog pounced on me at one point, and I slid under a chair for protection while Tom diverted his attention so I could escape. At first, the Poodle stood aside as if she didn't want to ruin those manicured nails of hers, but she couldn't resist joining the fracas for very long. She participated in the jaw sparring, air snapping, pushing and shoving with the rest of us. Even the Brittany gave up on the field issue and joined in the frivolity. The timid Beagle pup just stayed under a chair, and the Bassett Hound continued to cheer us on from the sidelines. By the time class was over, we were all exhausted. This Puppy Kindergarten stuff was really fun, and I couldn't wait until next week to do this all over again.

This fun activity dubbed Socialization Time continued for a few weeks along with some learning. We were introduced to a few other commands but had fun with variations of the SIT/DOWN/STAND combinations. After all, it was a school setting and not just a place to run rampant during play time. We also spent time learning how to walk properly on a leash. That was pretty comical since not one pup in the class demonstrated coordination or self-control while on the leash…myself included.

As we all grew taller, our friendships grew as well. The Poodle was quite the conversationalist, and the English Sheepdog was always ready with a joke. The Brittany stayed focused on potential field work and earned the admiration of the class. Tom and I thought we'd be friends forever since we had so much in common. Puppy Kindergarten sure was fun. School days were cool days!

Within a few weeks, we were ready for graduation. It was such a wonderful event. We had games, and I have to be truthful in that Tom beat me in the SIT/DOWN/STAND Competition by two seconds. Of course, he was a much smaller breed, had shorter legs and could reach the floor quicker, but I wasn't going to be a sore loser. I'd get him next time!

As the sounds of *Pomp and Circumstance* echoed from the portable tape recorder, we approached in a single line to accept our graduation certificates from the instructors. We were all now Puppy Kindergarten graduates and mighty proud of it.

Some of us were headed for Beginning Obedience Class. That sounded so special, and I couldn't wait for that class to start. Sure, it meant more learning, repetition of commands and probably more practice walking correctly on a leash, but the thought of play time at the end of the session made up for any work I might have to do while in the learning phase of the class.

Since my dad worked with me in Puppy Kindergarten, my mom took me to the Beginning Obedience Class; and to my dismay, there was no play time at the end of the class. It was strictly learning. We were told that we were too old for play time now. How could any puppy be too old for fun? Don't we need a lot of socialization in order to be well adjusted pups?

Tom was in my class along with the English Sheepdog; and while it was great to see them again, it just wasn't the same. Without the running, pushing and shoving at the end of the class, it was just learning. What fun was that? Maybe the next class would be different. One could always hope; and at this stage of my life, hope was now something to be enjoyed. However, nothing ever stays the same, and what came next was a real setback...

# 6

## Stuff Happens

As the weeks passed, the obedience classes became more challenging for me. I went from Beginning Obedience to the Intermediate Class which centered on basic commands and walking correctly on a leash. I was pretty good with the commands, but I still found proper leash behavior very challenging. Because everything around me was exciting, my need for exploration often found me tugging at the end of the leash. *Pop goes the correction* when that happened and my mom would change walking directions to regain my focus. Leash behavior was tough especially for a free spirit like myself.

Then, there was the socialization issue. There was no time for that in these classes. Without any play time, it was school without recess, and what fun was that? None of my friends from Puppy Kindergarten and Beginning Obedience were there. They were probably at home, being good pets, chewing on something or sleeping on their family's couches. That's what I call living the good life!

I didn't get to do any of those things...especially sleeping on the couch. Furniture was only for people in my house. I had very specific rules to follow at home because of my potential as an assistance dog, and learning was a daily process. I was pretty full of myself with all of this knowledge seeping into my brain. How much more could my brain hold? It seemed pretty full to me.

However, this assistance dog training stuff wasn't all just learning commands and following rules of behavior. The "Wearing of the Cape" was one of the highlights. Now, it doesn't look like the one Superman wears or any other action hero, but it is just as magical for me. While wearing that cape with ties around my chest and stomach, I stretched my imagination and became my own Super Action Hero. Look out Rin Tin Tin, Lassie and White Fang! Kessen, the Mighty Dog, is the new pup in town!

Wearing the cape wasn't always so exciting. I was introduced to it when I first came to live with my new family and wasn't particularly fond of it. It was like wearing a colorful napkin. What would that do to my image? Nevertheless, every day when it was training time, my mom would remind me that it was time to go to work She'd put the cape on me and was careful not to let the ties under my stomach stick out too much. I liked to chew on them when in a DOWN position.

*Those ties were so tasty.*

What I soon noticed was that people looked at me differently when I was wearing the cape. They weren't allowed to pet me since I was "working" which I didn't understand. Being in a DOWN position on the sidewalk seemed more like resting than working, but rules are rules. The people smiled, said kind words about me and commented on my cape. I wagged my tail in appreciation and realized that I must look pretty cool in this cape for them to take such special notice of me. In my mind, each day held the promise of adventures, and wearing my cape was the portal to my imagination.

*My cape was magical.*

As I grew taller and gained weight, I graduated to a larger cape with a buckle around the stomach. No more string ties for me to chew, but I had already lost interest in that activity a few weeks earlier. Although I still missed play time with other dogs, my life was good. Soon that would change.

In addition to my weekly obedience class, my mom took me to a monthly training session in a very large facility. At first, I wasn't too excited about the prospect of another training class; but since I had no say in the matter and got to wear my cape, I just went along with it. The cinder block walls of the facility had as much charm as a medieval dungeon, and only the front windows offered peeks into the outside world. No hope of any fun in this setting.

Then...I saw the other dogs. There were yellow and black Labrador Retrievers, Golden Retrievers and even mixes of the two breeds just like me. Some even had pink noses! My heart skipped a beat, and my mind went into overload. They were all wearing capes! This was not just a training class; it was a meeting of Super Action Heroes. My mind raced with the endless possibilities of what this adventure had to offer.

There were dogs of all ages and sizes in the group; but unlike my obedience classes, these dogs were all on track for being assistance dogs. Some were older and very advanced in terms of their learning curve. They probably knew just about everything there was to know...at least it looked that way to those of us who were much younger. They even walked nicely on a regulation leash while wearing a flat collar. That was a truly great accomplishment as far as I was concerned. They had perfect SITs, drop to the floor DOWNs and lengthy STAYs. Their behavior was definitely admired by the younger pups. We were in awe of their accomplishments, as well as the way they carried themselves while wearing their capes. I'm telling you, those capes had magical powers.

The other pups in the class, who were about my age, behaved mostly like me. They pulled on their leashes, had sloppy SITs, weren't comfortable being in a DOWN position on that floor with the strange residue in places, and preferred to get up rather than STAY in one position for any length of time. I guess the cape's magic had to develop gradually, and the meeting of the Super Action Heroes was really a training session in disguise.

Don't get the wrong impression. I wasn't opposed to learning...just the work involved in the process. I considered myself to be a *Sponge for Learning*. I willingly took it all in, but some things always slipped through the holes. My capacity for retaining information was limited due to my youth as well as my development of cranial matter. In everyday language, my puppy brain just couldn't handle all of the information in a timely manner. That's my story, and I'm sticking to it.

At the end of each monthly class, there was play time. I called it the icing on the treat bone. Our capes were removed, and the FREE command sent us running all over the place. We chased each other, jumped, rolled around and had the best time until our tongues were dragging. I was usually at the head of the pack in these play sessions; but in this particular class, I found that my hind legs just weren't keeping up with my front legs. It never happened before, or so I thought, but my mom noticed this right away. A look of concern washed over her face. She stopped me in mid-play before I had a real chance to burn off some of my excess energy, and I didn't know why.

The next day, my mom took me on yet another field trip to the animal hospital to be examined by a young and ever so lovely veterinarian. Apparently, my mom had recently seen this leg action once before while I was running around the yard and relayed this information to the veterinarian. The examination began; and while she was carefully rotating my hind legs, the doctor thought she heard a popping sound in my hip. Judging from her face, this was not a good sign...especially for a pup whose future might be assistance oriented. Sometimes, stuff just happens.

While there was no clear diagnosis due to my young age and newly developing bones, it was suggested that for the

next two months, I was not to run, jump or play with other dogs. I could walk for brief periods but nothing stressful. This was not good news for me at all. I was a free spirit who thrived on every opportunity to run amuck. The next two months were not going to be easy for me.

*I can't come out to play today.*

63

Leaving the animal hospital with a daily supplement for my bones, a dismal view of my next few weeks and the promise of some form of future evaluation, we made our way home. I had a major pity party, and to make it even worse was the fact that I couldn't even invite my friends.

*Oh, woe is me.*

This hip popping possibility was definitely a setback for me, yet one that I couldn't have anticipated. I was a young and strong pup on my way to a great future. On any other day, having four legs and silent hips is a distinct advantage. Thanks to the possible syncopation in my hip, today was not one of them.

The days passed slowly; and while I was still learning things on a daily basis as well as taking my walks, I was losing a vital part of my development...my ability to relate to other dogs in play situations.

*He's my only playmate these days.*

My mom, being exceptionally introspective, recognized this and told me that she had another remedy in her Tool Box of Tricks to help with this deficiency. (*She had a tool box?*) She told me that she was calling in the Big Guns! I didn't have a clue as to what that meant; but once again judging from past experiences, I was in for a really big surprise. However, nothing I had ever encountered prepared me for what was to come...

7

# Puppy Etiquette

I was now six months old and still under doctor's orders regarding play. My only source of entertainment was learning new commands, reviewing what I had learned, participating in obedience classes and taking daily walks in the neighborhood. There was no reason for a ticker tape parade at this point in time.

However, today was my two month hip evaluation and, as it turned out, was my date with destiny. On the way to the animal hospital, my imagination ran wild with anticipation and apprehension. Additionally, I was forced to fight against my ever present fear of looking out the car windows, so I wrapped myself around one of my toys, hugged the crate's floor and conjured up my mantra for courage for this doctor's evaluation. POWER TO THE PUP resonated in my brain, and the "what ifs" of my situation periodically interrupted my mantra causing me to lose focus. What if my hip still popped? What if I never played with other dogs again or regained the freedom to run amuck in the yard?

Truth be told, those weren't even the worst of my fears. My biggest fear, aside from the car window phobia, was that I might not be able to continue my training as a potential assistance dog. In spite of the way I carried on about the boredom of obedience classes and the difficulty of learning without recess, the prospect of a career in service intrigued me in ways I didn't quite understand. Maybe the prospect of wearing a cape on a daily basis led me to believe that a dog in uniform was, by nature, irresistible to the female canine population. That, plus the tattoo in my ear, made for a real chick magnet. Was my convoluted logic a blessing or a curse?

Besides, it was out of my paws at this point and in the hands of the veterinarian's evaluation.

There were no animals in the waiting room at the animal hospital, and my name was called right away. My mom, dad and I had serious looks on our faces when the doctor came into the examination room. My veterinarian had the bluest eyes and was the prettiest doctor I had ever seen. Could someone so attractive be the bearer of bad news? I hoped not. Silence filled the room as she examined me and slowly rotated my hind legs. I was almost afraid to breathe in case she would mistake that for the sound of popping. When she finished, she flashed a huge smile. No popping in my hip could be heard anymore. Bark, howl and screech…treats are on the house! I was once again off the disabled list and free to run, play hearty and have a good time with other dogs.

I hadn't played with other dogs for over two months now, but back then I was a rough player. I wasn't much of a puppy anymore, had grown into my wrinkles as well as my hamburger patty-sized paws. Strong, perfectly straight teeth replaced my razor sharp puppy teeth, and I had gained some weight. I had long, lanky legs, but my nose hadn't turned pink yet. Maybe it wouldn't; but even if it did, I'd handle it. I was still somewhat of a hunk…if you know what I mean. How would I now hold up in play against the grown up dogs? After all, I was out of practice for a while and may have lost my edge on the playground of socialization skills.

Leave it to my mom to plan ahead. She had already made arrangements to deal with a possible deficiency in my socialization techniques. After all, she had seen me in action before with other dogs, and she was bringing in the Big Guns to make it all happen. I didn't know what to expect. How could Big Guns help me in my quest to regain socialization skills? It just didn't make sense to me.

About a week later, my mom's plan came together with the ringing of our front door bell. Since I had an assigned spot to sit when the doorbell rang, I immediately assumed that position. Were these the Big Guns my mom talked about? What was a Big Gun anyway? The anticipation was almost too much for me to bear. I squirmed from excitement, and my typical sloppy SIT was even sloppier from the anticipation of what was behind Door Number One.

As the door slowly opened, my questions were quickly answered. In walked the most magnificent looking Golden Retriever I had ever seen. He was tall, had a long flowing, honey colored coat and the markings of a white mask surrounded his eyes and muzzle. Regal wasn't even a close description of this dog. As he carefully surveyed the room, his penetrating eyes locked in on my face; and due to my immaturity, my first thoughts turned to SLEEPOVER! The Big Guns weren't guns at all. It was a dog brought here for fun and games. Canines, start your engines!

I couldn't contain myself any longer. I leapt from my assigned spot and jumped all over this gorgeous canine as a way of welcoming him to our house. With an action faster than the speed of light, this invited guest let loose with a quiver of his lips, a low growl and a muffled snap that made the sleepover idea seem a bit premature in terms of fun. His barred teeth came so close to my face that I might have been able to count his teeth had I not been so shocked. With my head down and tail tucked, I quickly withdrew backwards from him, and I didn't even know that I could walk backwards! (*How did he do that with his lips?*)

I was totally confused and looked at my mom as if to question her intent as well as the usefulness of this so called tool from her Tool Box. Seeing my speedy retreat from this new arrival, she gave me the clarification I needed...Our visitor's name was Linus, and he specialized in the socialization of overly enthusiastic pups. (*It was a nice way of saying rowdy.*) His job was to help me to readjust to the canine community in a polite and proper manner. In other words, Linus was a teacher of Puppy Etiquette; and his lip quiver, low growl and muffled snap became his Three Step Action Plan.

My suspicious nature took over, and I felt the need for more information…especially after his less than grand entrance. I questioned his credentials since I never heard of a dog doing this line of work. Where did he go to school for this, what were his grades, did he graduate at the top of his class and if so, what was his class rank? I needed answers, especially after his not so friendly entrance to our house. I sensed that I wasn't going to get any information now. His owner gave my mom his overnight bag containing his food and left us to get acquainted. Apparently, it was going to be a sleepover after all, but not quite the one I had in mind.

Perhaps Linus and I just started out on the wrong paw and could start over. After all, he was a visitor in our house, and I was taught to be respectful of guests. As I approached him again, I playfully bumped his side and did a bit of a twirl as a sign of friendship. Once again, I was at the critical end his Three Step Action Plan. What was wrong with this dog? Those teeth barely missed me! What good was looking so very magnificent if you didn't have a sense of humor?

Then, he spoke. "Look here, Bud. What kind of greeting was that? I'd say you were raised by wolves, but that would give wolves a bad name." Following that, he found a comfortable spot on the carpet.

The audacity of this dog, this so-called Puppy Etiquette Teacher, to question my upbringing was unbelievable! We'll see how this all plays out.

Linus went on to explain that there were certain rules of behavior in the canine world, and he would stay at our house until I not only learned them but practiced them as well. He was a dog of few words and all action. I thought that I was pompous!

Our lessons began immediately with proper greetings. Approaching from the side was acceptable since frontal greetings with direct eye contact were confrontational. Jumping all over another dog was just unacceptable and rude. Since when? I've been doing that for six months. From behind me, I heard him say, "Since now."

Linus was all over me like a tick on an unprotected pooch. He used that lip quiver, low growl and muffled snap any chance he could. He made sure that he ate first while I stood and watched. He had free access to my toys without question, and my total submission was confirmed by my walking behind him at all times. This wasn't a sleepover. It was Boot Camp, and it lasted for days.

Yet, I wasn't getting discouraged, and my lack of common sense led me to believe that deep down, Linus knew how to have a good time. Our living room had the layout of a perfect running track, and I displayed my racing ability by running around the room. At first, I lumbered around my imaginary track and then gradually increased my speed. Linus watched carefully; and in my limited capacity for realistic thought, I actually believed that he was about to join in the fun. How wrong must I be, and how many times being wrong would it take for me to gain some common sense?

Linus did not join in the race. Instead, he blocked one corner of my path, and his quivering lip, low growl and muffled snap brought me skidding to a stop. I quickly reversed my course and was off again. Then, he slowly walked to the other corner…once again blocking my path. He did this effortless maneuver over and over again until I just gave up. Apparently, *No Running in the House* was another rule of puppy etiquette. Mr. Take Away the Fun was at the top of his game. There had to be some venue for fun; and since the house was off limits, it must be the yard. It was too soon to tell.

I already learned not to jump on him and above all, not to touch his stomach. What's with the stomach? Linus explained that the Stomach Rule only applied to him. He never told me why; and after the few days of his schooling, I learned not to question Mr. Pompous, as I called him behind his back. I danced around him, twirled, bowed to engage him in play as he taught me the day before and got absolutely no response from him. Evidently, *Having Patience* was another rule of puppy etiquette. We never did play that day. It was just another exercise in futility.

After a few days of imposed instruction and repeated use of his Three Step Action Plan, I found myself doing the things that Linus taught me without even thinking about them. I no longer cared that he ate his meals first or that he grabbed any of my toys...even if one was still in my mouth. As he walked through the house, I fell into step behind him without any thought whatsoever. I now knew how to greet other dogs politely and what was expected of me...not only in the house in terms of behavior but also in playing with other dogs as well.

*Linus was tough...but fair.*

On the last day of Linus' extended sleepover, we went into the yard for what I thought might be the last rule of puppy etiquette. In his highbrow, instructional tone, he informed me that a canine never stopped learning. Oh boy…Mr. Pompous was back! Anyway, I thought it would go just as the other days had gone…I'd bow and beg for any attempt at play, and Linus would just ignore my efforts.

However, the surprise was on me. As we went out to the yard together, Linus turned to me and bowed as only a member of the monarchy might bow. In one graceful and flowing movement, he was engaging me in play. *Me?* I turned around to see if his bow was meant for some other dog behind me, but realized his actions were directed at me. Yikes! Was this a trick? Being a risk taker, I took the chance and returned the bow. There were no tricks today. Linus finally granted me an opportunity to play. Off we went, running circles around each other and making paths through the bushes. That dog could run!

We had the best time in the yard; and when exhaustion set in, we laid in the cool grass for a while. Linus reminded me of everything he taught me and what was expected in terms of being a responsible canine. I finally understood that everything he did these past few days was meant not to punish but to instruct. He was, indeed, a teacher of Puppy

Etiquette. While I still had a lot to learn, Linus had taught me the basics.

Before Linus left that day, my mom wanted to take a picture of us together…teacher and student etched into digital history. As she aimed the camera at us, I flashed my most attractive smile; and in that second, Linus turned his face away. It seems he didn't like his picture taken and refused any further attempts to capture the moment. Was he afraid of the camera? While I thought that was pretty funny, Linus reminded me of my car window phobia. Touché! That was enough about phobias.

As Linus made his way to his owner's car, I knew I was going to miss him. Days went by, and I tried to duplicate his lip quiver; but the attempts only tickled me, and the resulting laughter didn't have the same daunting effect. I guess it was something to be developed as I matured.

Linus did come to stay with us a few more times in the years to come, especially when we had potential assistance puppies in the house. I was sure to be on my best behavior and put my best paws forward when he was around. I didn't want him to think that I had forgotten what he had taught me. I also didn't want to be the recipient of his Three Step Action Plan for puppy correction. While he always came close with those hazardous teeth, he never made contact. I wanted that record to remain solidly on the books. On his last visit, Linus allowed my mom to take his picture and I do believe that he posed for the camera.

*Linus…my favorite teacher.*

Years later, I learned that Linus had passed on to the Rainbow Bridge and was enjoying the peace and happiness promised to animals in the afterlife. He would no longer offer his wisdom to overly enthusiastic pups as he did for me. It was such a tremendous loss for the canine world. Linus did what no other human trainer could do…he taught dogs how to be respectful animals as only a dog could teach that to another dog. Furthermore, he did it with finesse and style.

I was never able to master his Three Step Action Plan for teaching Puppy Etiquette. There was something about that lip quiver combined with the low growl and muffled snap that just didn't come together for me. It might have been the laughter from the lip tickling that prevented my successful execution of the plan. However, that lack of success was fitting since no other dog would ever come close to duplicating the skills demonstrated by Linus.

I never did thank him for everything he had done for me; and sadly, I wished that I had not missed that opportunity. Everything he taught me was preparation for what was to occur in the coming months. It was the beginning of a chain reaction of events that would ultimately change the direction of my life...

**8**

# Going Public

For as long as I can remember, I was told that someday I might be an assistance dog and all of my training was geared toward that goal. Sometime in the future, I would go off to a place called Puppy College, learn more commands and put my training to work. Having a job wasn't necessarily a goal of mine, but I'd give it my best shot. It might just be another opportunity to strut my stuff, and I pictured myself as a potential Big Dog on the Kennel Campus at Puppy College.

In the meantime, major consideration was given to socializing, learning the appropriate commands and behaving properly on the leash. Thanks to Linus, my socialization skills were improved; thanks to my mom and dad, my efforts in terms of commands were on track. However, my leash behavior left a lot to be desired. It just wasn't my thing. Once I realized that I had control of this, I decided I would just take my time mastering the skill. One day in the near future, I'd kick it up a notch, surprise the folks and consistently walk nicely on the leash. At least in that area, I had the upper paw.

All that was left in my training was the public etiquette phase, and that wasn't anything learned in the classroom or taught by another dog. Actual experience in the world outside of my neighborhood was needed. I wasn't sure what to expect or when it would begin. I just knew it was coming. As it turned out, going public came much sooner than I expected.

I was changing in so many ways. My cape and collars were now a size larger; and as I continued to grow, I barely recognized myself. Every day it seemed as though something was either getting bigger or wider on me. I was only getting two meals a day now, and the folks were still trying to fool me into thinking that the morsels for doing good things were additional treats. I had known for quite a while that those so-called treats were actually parts of my breakfast and dinner, but it did take a while before I caught on to their tactic. Some days, I just wasn't at my peak performance level...others, I was at the top of my game. Consistency wasn't one of my strengths.

The air bristled with excitement on this particular day, and I didn't know why. My travel bag was packed with a water bowl, water bottle, paper towels, poop bags, treat pouch, camera and identification cards. The packing was standard for a field trip, but the destination was still unknown. Hopefully, it was somewhere that offered the opportunity for play time, and I never passed up an opportunity for that. Then, I saw my mom put my cape at the top of my travel bag. My cape? I never wore my cape on a field trip, so this had to be extra special. My spirit of adventure and active imagination went into overdrive with her words that were music to my ears. Today, I was going public!

Yikes! Public! I had been training for this day for months but never had any warning that it would be today. I'd make my first public appearance at some place outside of my typical, little world; and apparently, I was dressing for the occasion. Look out world...Kessen, the Mighty Dog, was hitting the pavement.

I was now big enough to get into the car by myself; and once in the back seat, I jumped enthusiastically into my canvas crate. Because I still had the car window phobia, I immediately dropped into a sloppy, prone position on the crate's floor. Why was I still afraid of looking out of car windows? To settle my nerves, I conjured up my POWER TO THE PUP mantra. This was my first public appearance, and my goal was to make a good impression.

When we reached our destination, my mom put the cape on me, attached my leash and gave me permission to leave the car. It was my moment…the step into the history book of my life. With my mom and dad walking on either side of me, I strutted across the parking lot. Just as I was taught, I came to a complete stop followed by a perfect sitting position. Usually my SITs bordered on sloppy, but today, I had been at my personal best. It was time to get the camera. Directly in front of me was my destiny…it was the bagel restaurant!

While I spent some time greeting people in front of the restaurant, my dad grabbed the camera from my travel bag and shifted it in all directions to accurately record this special moment. As people stopped to pet me before they entered the restaurant, I could tell that I was developing quite a fan base. It had to be the magic of the cape. Who would have thought it would also be a magnet for people? I wasn't just a dog; I was a dog in uniform! They couldn't wait to pet me as Kessen, the Mighty Dog, worked the crowd. This attention was a colossal boost to my ego...as if my ego needed any boosting. If my head got any bigger from the praise and petting, they'd have to enlarge the doorways for my head to fit through them. From past experience with fence rails, I already knew my head size meant trouble. Somehow, this was different.

Just when I thought that this going public gig couldn't get any better, I had an even bigger surprise. We were now actually going to go inside the restaurant. *INSIDE!* As I waited at the threshold of the entrance door for my command to proceed, the significance of this moment registered in my mind. While this was one small step for me, it was a giant step for the canine world. Could I be any more dramatic?

My heart beat steadily as I crossed the threshold of the front door. Making my grand entrance, I watched as heads turned, conversations stopped and all attention was on me. This was definitely my kind of gig. I'm sure they wondered what such a good looking dog, wearing a cape, was doing in the restaurant. Since this was my first public outing, I hadn't reached my full celebrity status except, of course, in my mind.

I only had a taste of that status at the front door with my newly discovered fans.

I was jolted back to reality upon hearing someone say that I must be a service dog in training and was learning to assist people. Was it my handsome appearance, my confident demeanor, or was it the magic of the cape directing the people in the restaurant to the proper conclusion? I couldn't tell, but they just nodded approval to each other and resumed eating their meals.

Now, that response might have sufficed for some dogs, but this just wasn't a successful follow up to the outdoor welcome from my fans. My moment came and went in an instant. I was lucky I didn't blink, or I would have missed it. Was that it? Where was the applause or the requests for pictures and pawtographs? (*Since I couldn't write, pawtographs would have to do.*) To say the least, the lack of total appreciation for my being there was a bit of a letdown for me. There had to be more to this public appearance gig.

My mom and dad took me to a table at the far end of the restaurant, and I was given my command to go UNDER. *Under? Under the table?* How was I supposed to see everything there was to see in this new place from that position? I was definitely relegated to the cheap seats, and all I could see were legs from the knees down and very small children. This certainly wasn't what I expected, but I figured out a way to make the best of it. My mom wasn't the only one with a Tool Box of Tricks.

Since situational awareness was one of my many tools, I relied on that for the execution of my plan. I closely surveyed the area and determined that if I slowly inched toward the end of the table, I'd eventually have a much better view of my surroundings. Moving two or three inches would accomplish my goal of an unobstructed view. Not even the aroma of freshly baked bagels and muffins interfered with my plan. Like a stealth bomber, I discreetly began inching my way towards a better view...actually thinking that my actions would be undetected by either my mom or dad. Faster than a tick jumping on a pooch, I was tactfully reprimanded. *Pop goes the correction!* Apparently, not enough thought was put into that endeavor.

Nevertheless, I wasn't one to give up. Pretending to demonstrate a more professional looking position on the floor, I shifted my body a few times and in doing that, actually moved a bit closer to the end of the table. I was definitely a smooth operator, and now I had a clear view of the restaurant. I finally had a plan that worked. My confidence level soared. Today, Kessen, the Mighty Dog, was at his peak performance level.

Basking in the glory of my accomplishment, I was now content with my role as a silent guardian and observer. People came and went...chomping away on their food and enjoying conversations with each other. While the aromas of the bagels and the muffins eventually caused a bit of drooling on my part, I was rewarded with periodic bits of my breakfast disguised as treats. That was meant to reinforce my good behavior. Did it get any better than this? I was getting rewards for just lying under a table and being quiet. If this were considered work, I'm all for joining the work force. Going public was a breeze!

Before we left, the manager of the restaurant came over to the table, complimented my behavior and told my folks that I was welcome to visit any time. My mom and dad praised me a lot for being such a good dog. I felt a little guilty because I deceived them in order to find a better view from under the table, but guilt is a wasted emotion. At least that's what my mom said once. Today, I followed her advice, shook off the guilt and basked in the glow of my first, successful visit to the public arena. Having a plan that actually worked was also something to celebrate.

From that day on, I went just about everywhere with Mom and Dad. Since I wore my cape and had papers to prove I was in training for service, I had quite a variety of experiences. When we visited a place for the first time, we sat near an exit door just in case a quick departure was necessary. Let's face it. There were new sights and sounds every place we went. Expectations of me were high, and my folks couldn't know my reactions to new stimuli. I wasn't much of a barker, but they took their chances every time we went somewhere new. Being near an exit door was their safety net, and at times, it was mine as well.

I became a regular at church every Sunday and went to the early service because the church wasn't filled to capacity at that time of the morning. At first, we sat all the way in the back so I got a feel for the place, the sights and the sounds. Eventually, we worked our way to the middle but always at the end of the pew...just in case. The choir's melodies were soothing to me. Because I was in a DOWN position most of the time and couldn't see anything but the backs of people's shoes, I relied on my sense of hearing for satisfaction. Since I wasn't much of a morning dog, I was content with that. Catching a few extra winks during the service was a bonus. Belching and loud yawning was frowned upon. On one occasion, I tried drinking from the Holy Water Fountain as we passed it on our way out of the church. Let me put it this way...I only tried that once.

For the next six months, my mom and dad took me to all kinds of places. We became regulars at the bagel restaurant and made field trips to shopping malls where I learned to ride up and down on the elevators. It took me longer to get used to the ones with glass walls, but eventually I did. We made our way through department stores, grocery stores, the library, the hardware store, the train station, schools, health care offices and so many other public places. Each new place or situation had its own version of challenges, but some were easier to overcome than others.

Experiencing a variety of surfaces was also part of my training. I walked on concrete, asphalt, dirt, sand, grass, mulch, over metal grates and even bubble wrap just to get used to the differences. I thought that the bubble wrap was meant to throw me off my game, but it didn't. I got used to the popping sounds under the weight of my body and pretended I could walk on it all day. Who was I fooling? While I hate to admit this, it took me quite a few tries to cross a wooden bridge that spanned a narrow brook. The uneven planks felt rough on the pads of my paws, and the sound of the rushing water underneath the bridge was unsettling. My trusty mantra, POWER TO THE PUP, helped me to get to the other side and back. Then, I did it again, and the task got a bit easier. I never felt totally comfortable crossing that bridge and hoped that I wouldn't have to do it very often.

Shiny floors are often very slippery, so caution, slow walking and neatly trimmed nails are a necessity. Stairs are also a challenge since the tendency for me is to race to the top just to get there and do the same on the reverse trip. Consequently, I had to learn to walk up and down one step at a time. It wasn't easy especially if the stairs had open railings like the ones at the high school. I'll admit that I wasn't very good at it, but I tried. I never got that quite right since my tendency was to race up and down just to get it done.

Mom and Dad even took me to the movies a few times. We sat really close to the screen because that's where I would sit if I became an assistance dog. Everything on the screen was so big from where we sat, but I had the best time whenever we went. I particularly enjoyed seeing the movie, *Flicka,* which was about a beautiful horse and the person who loved her. Being a romantic at heart, I was mesmerized by the story as well as by the periodic bits of popcorn that my dad slipped to me. I loved that popcorn!

*Paw Lickin' Good!*

*The Illusionist* was another adventure at the movies, but it didn't hold my interest as well as the story about *Flicka*; probably because it cut into my meal time. Eating was and is one of my priorities, and everything else takes a back seat to meal time.

There was so much to learn, and I didn't know if my head, although physically large in size, would hold it all. My folks covered as much as they could in order to prepare me for Puppy College, and believe me, they accomplished a lot in the six months after my going public for the first time. They made sure that I worked at my own pace and never rushed me into situations if I demonstrated any sort of apprehension. While I was grateful for that, I had some doubts as to whether or not I was cut out for this line of work.

When in public, the attention centered on me, and that definitely appealed to my celebrity image. However, nagging doubts entered my brain, and I just didn't know if this line of work was right for me. While I did look forward to going to Puppy College, it meant leaving people who loved me unconditionally. They consistently ignored my screw ups but never missed an opportunity to praise good behavior...even if it were for something as trivial as a perfect SIT. They asked so little of me yet tolerated so much.

How could I leave these wonderful folks and the life they gave me? Was questioning my future role due to the inherent responsibility of the job, or because I'd have to leave my home where life was easy and uncomplicated? Let's face it. I didn't have the best track record in terms of mature decision making.

*Seemed like a good idea.*

How could I help someone else when on most days, I couldn't help myself?

I didn't know where I was headed. What I did know was that at this moment in time, I reveled in my celebrity status, enjoyed most of the new experiences and tried to put a positive spin on future plans. However, I soon learned that going public meant a lot more than just being the center of attention, behaving appropriately and making a good impression. What happened next as part of my going public gig was beyond my expectations. It was Showtime...

93

9

# Demo Dog

While going out in public was exciting, it included more than just looking good and behaving appropriately. What began as a regular training exercise turned into increased notoriety for me and definitely broadened my fan base. Kessen, the Mighty Dog, was destined for stardom...not just in the public eye, but on the stage as well. However, my first stage appearance was in a most unlikely place.

Part of my public experiences involved visiting schools. The shiny floors offered opportunities for cautious walking, and the stairs, with their open railings, gave me experience in one step at a time training. Traveling in the halls with students offered the opportunity to walk among crowds as well as practice greetings. Schools had all of the elements of a well-rounded training facility.

My dad had been a guidance counselor at a high school for many years. As a result, he had connections in getting permission for me to practice my skills...or lack of them. To prevent me from being overwhelmed, my mom and dad took me to the high school after classes were finished for the day. We walked the halls slowly and went up and down those dreaded, open stairs. Our last stop was the Guidance Office. Guidance counselors, some teachers and a few students awaited my arrival for practice with greetings.

Since I wore my cape, everything was considered a training exercise. Greetings had to be appropriate, and there would be no jumping, licking or rolling around the floor. Those were my rules and not the greeters.

The protocol for greetings was to ask permission of my handler to greet, allow me to sniff their hand, pet me under my chin and then step back. If I moved from my sitting position, the greeting started all over again. There wasn't a whole lot of loving going on and definitely no need to call in ushers to control the crowds. They weren't rushing to greet me, but I didn't mind. Even though greetings were formal, they were still attention. If one stretched the imagination, it was still positive attention, and who doesn't like that?

My mom always carried brochures about assistance dogs and on that first visit, she gave out quite a few of them. Both teachers and students were interested in what I was being trained to do. One of the teachers asked if we could visit her classroom to talk about me and my training. Talk about ME? Just tell me where and when, and I'd be there. The subject I knew best was ME!

Little did I know that my celebrity status was about to be upgraded to first class. I was on a rocket to stardom and didn't even know it. I wasn't discovered in a bagel shop while resting quietly under a table. Once permission for my visit was given, my flight to stardom began in a high school classroom.

On the day of my first demo, my mom made sure that I was clean, well brushed and prepared. As I gazed at my reflection in the patio door, I noticed that at some time during the past few weeks, my nose had changed colors. It wasn't pink, but a color close to dusty rose. That shade really complimented my deep brown eyes and golden coat. I thought I was definitely going to make a good impression.

My travel bag was stocked with the appropriate items, my cape was just washed and my dad got the canvas crate in the car ready for me. Off we went. My rocket to stardom was on the launch pad, and the countdown had begun.

Walking through the school was wonderful. With my head held high and my tail at full wagging capacity, I didn't know what I was doing or where I was going. My confidence had soared with each past experience, and I could always ad lib if necessary. Heads turned when the students saw me walking through the halls, and their *oohs* and *aahs* made my heart beat a bit faster. This was another moment for me to increase my fan base. Having paws prevented me from a full, frontal wave, so I flashed my best smile. That would have to do for now.

As we got closer to the classroom, I heard music, and it sounded like marching music. The beat was exhilarating; and the closer we got, the louder the sound became. Did they hire a band for my arrival? What a wonderful welcome! As it turned out, the Pep Band was just practicing for the next football game, and the music had nothing to do with my arrival. Maybe next time, when my fame preceded me, the music would be for me.

After traveling up those dreaded stairs, we reached the classroom, and I sat quietly while we waited for permission to enter. This was my classroom debut and my first captive audience. My mom kissed me on the top of my head and wished me luck. Luck? Luck had nothing to do with it. It all depended on style and finesse...I had both.

I walked in to my first demonstration with my head held high and my tail wagging. Once again, the *oohs* and *aahs* of my audience were music to my floppy ears. This music wasn't at all like the band music I heard earlier, but I could listen to this type of music all day long. My mom was my warm up act. For obvious reasons, she did all of the talking in this phase. I would do the legwork in the middle, and my dad would give resource information at the end. It was a well planned demonstration.

Background information about my coming from California was given, and my command list was discussed. Mom also talked about the significance of the cape in terms of a working dog, as well as how public experiences prepared me for my future role as an assistance dog. My mom even thanked them for assisting in my training by allowing me to visit their classroom. (*Who would have thought my mom knew how to work a room?*) I was impressed! She seemed to have their full attention.

My mom gave a lot of information, and the students were really interested in the whole process of a dog becoming an assistance dog. I anxiously awaited my turn on the classroom stage, and then it came. I stood at attention in the front of the class and executed a perfect SIT. There were no sloppy paws here today. I then demonstrated my DOWN, STAND, STAY, the dreaded UNDER (*the one that hinders all views*), FORWARD and BACK. I actually learned how to walk backwards since Linus' Three Step Action Plan forced me into walking backwards. Nowadays, I didn't do it out of fear. I did it because I was trained to do it since it might be necessary to walk backwards in front of a wheel chair while going through a narrow door way.

The class loved that move and my tail just kept wagging as they watched my performance. I did the LAP command where I laid across my mom's lap; it was a comfort position for my handler as well as a way for someone to rest their hands or balance a book for reading on my back. For whatever reason, I stayed there until given my OFF command. I also liked the SPEAK command since I could demonstrate my velvet-toned voice. Unfortunately, I was only allowed to bark once because a proper assistance dog can't be barking up a storm. For some dogs, the One Bark Rule is difficult. It wasn't for me, but I think it's because I am somewhat lazy; and past experience with barking had only proven to be an exercise in futility. My audience was impressed with my self-control, but they didn't know the real reasons for my adherence to the One Bark Rule.

Retrieval of dropped objects would be another important aspect of my job, so I picked up a cell phone, a TV remote, a wallet, keys, an envelope and a pencil. The class was mesmerized.

The grand finale was a demonstration of my UP/SHAKE commands. I stood UP with my front paws on the wall and with the SHAKE command, turned off the lights with my paw. I heard all of the OMG's from the students. My star had risen, and I no longer was Kessen, the Mighty Dog...I was Kessen, the Demo Dog. My path to stardom was paved with students' smiles of appreciation and approval.

My dad then followed up with resource information and how others might become puppy raisers for potential assistance dogs. Material was distributed, and then anyone who was interested could greet me. They followed the procedure: ask permission of the handler, allow to sniff, pet under the chin and step back. To my surprise, everyone wanted to do it. I was overwhelmed by their kindness.

After everyone had greeted me, my mom again thanked the class for their attention as well as for their help in my training. This was my first demonstration; and as the class applauded, my mom gave me my BOW command. This was not one of my required commands, but one that she thought was cool. I deliberately put my front paws forward in what I considered my best bow ever. In the most unlikely of places, a high school classroom, I became a star...Kessen, the Demo Dog, was in the building!

Surprisingly, this one classroom demonstration led to a total of seventeen classroom demonstrations within a three week period. Word spread, and the requests came pouring in for demonstrations. I became a regular at the school, and the students no longer gave their *oohs* and *aahs* when they saw me but called me by name as I passed by. While I periodically heard the Pep Band playing, I knew it wasn't for me. Truth be told, I pretended it was, and it couldn't get any better than that. Being a Demo Dog was such a fantastic gig.

I had great fun at the high school except for the dreaded open railings on the stairs. The students and staff were fantastic each time we visited. It wasn't so much a measure of a fan base as it was students who enjoyed seeing me, greeting me or learning about what I was to do when I grew up. Wasn't that what they were learning to do in high school? Actually, we were all very much the same except for body types and capacity for learning. There is a lot more to it, but my point is that we are all trying to find our way in the world.

Many demonstrations followed after that first high school gig. We took our show on the road to numerous other schools, Dog Walks, Pet Shows, Rotary breakfasts, Assisted Living Facilities and even a music recital.

I fooled around a lot while my mom talked. It was my way of seeking attention. I chewed on her shoe strings while she talked or pulled the table cloth almost off the edge of the table while she accepted a hefty Rotary donation to the service dog organization. I felt that it was all in fun, and my shenanigans kept her on her toes when with me. Since she believed in rewarding the good behavior and ignoring the bad, I had an open door to mischief. I'm not proud that I took advantage of her training philosophy; but being in the public eye on a daily basis was sometimes stressful, and my goofing off was also a way for me to unwind from the stresses of the day.

We had a gig in a church once. The goal was to have the parishioners recognize the need for more accommodations for the challenged members of their community. They needed better chairs, ramps and easier access to the church. My mom centered her talk on those objectives and how the church community might bond together to make the church more accessible to those who face challenges on a daily basis. She was very informative and even had me going for a while. Did I sit there looking attentive to her words? Unfortunately, I chose the road not followed by the wise. I deliberately chewed on my mom's shoe laces while she talked. At one point, I had one completely untied.

During this presentation, my mom was wearing one of those portable microphones and couldn't afford to give me any verbal correction that might resonate through the church. It might not look very good to yank the collar of the potential assistance dog in a correction either...especially if you wanted them to give graciously for accessibility improvements. She just kept on talking about the needs of the church community and how their challenged members might best be served. No attention whatsoever was given to my shenanigans. I eventually stopped chewing and started to pay attention. I guess her methods worked after all.

The church community did eventually make their church more accessible in terms of ramps and cushioned chairs. While I learned that goofing off might get attention for a moment, the reputation of not goofing off lasted a whole lot longer. Wisdom comes not only with age but experience. That doesn't sound like me at all!

I learned a lot during those demonstrations, and each one was very different from the previous one. My mom made it exciting; I did the magic with my fancy paw work and my dad brought it all together with the finale of resource information.

*No more goofing off.*

We were quite the team, and all of our work resulted in well-earned vacation time, and that included what became my magnificent obsession...

# 10

# Water World

There is nothing more refreshing on a hot day than a drink of cold water…thirst quenching and lip smacking good! While supervised from the other side of the yard, I was allowed to run off leash and had many opportunities to create a parched throat. I played rough and hard with imaginary foes lurking behind bushes and shrubs. Someone watching might have thought something was wrong with me since no one else was in the yard chasing me or springing out from behind the shrubbery, but I didn't care. After getting my head caught in the fence rails when I was very young, embarrassing moments didn't faze me anymore. Following some of my misadventures, I was the first to laugh at myself and question my decision making skills.

This particular day ignited an obsession in me that I never saw coming or imagined. It started out like any other day with a visit to the bagel restaurant for public practice and then some free time in the yard. The weather was warm, and my fighting off imaginary foes was exhausting. After a while, my dad dragged a huge, yellow, circular container from the garage into the yard and then brought out the hose. In the past, I usually jumped at the water as it sprang from the hose. I twisted and turned in midair in an attempt to grab a mouthful of water, but the combination of the hose and the yellow object really fascinated me. My inquiring mind left the imaginary villains behind and instead investigated this new and unusual happening.

My dad started filling the circular container with water from the hose. Since I usually jumped at the water as it jettisoned from the hose, this entire scenario baffled me. I just watched and waited. My drooling response took over; and while I controlled myself, it was like seeing an oasis in the desert just a few paws away from my grasp. Then it hit me. This must be an outdoor water bowl! What will they think of next? I approached the huge, water-filled bowl with caution and tentatively lapped up some of the refreshing water. Oh, what a welcomed relief it was.

This next action was totally unexpected. Dad threw a rubber ball into the water bowl and said, "Kessen, GO GET." *GO GET?* What was he asking me to do? First of all, why did he throw the ball into the water bowl? He never did that to my water bowl in the house. Secondly, if I understood correctly, I was to jump into this water bowl to retrieve the ball. It just didn't make sense to me. However, my response to commands at this point in my training was greater than my confusion; so I jumped into the water. As bizarre as the request seemed, the outcome felt wonderful as I splashed around trying to get hold of the rubber ball. I'd take a little drink of the water and go back to my diving for the ball. It was such fun and totally refreshing, but I still couldn't get a grip on that ball!

My attempts to grasp that ball were not successful since the rubber was difficult to hold on to while wet. I resorted to my canine ingenuity to solve this problem. Since I enjoyed kicking up grass with my hind legs in the yard, why wouldn't it work with water? I vigorously began emptying the water bowl using my hind legs.

*I'm going to get that ball!*

I kicked and splashed water all over the place. When the bowl was almost empty of water, I gingerly picked up the ball and brought it to my dad. He just laughed at my cleverness and praised me for my dedication to a task. What a guy!

He brought the outdoor water bowl into the yard a lot after that first time. He'd fill it and drop that rubber ball smack dab into the center of the swirling water. I'd first spend some time jumping in and out trying to grab the slippery ball with my mouth. After numerous futile attempts, I'd empty the water bowl of its contents using my hind legs, and then grab the rubber ball and run. Sometimes, the ball would get kicked out with the water. It was all so much fun.

*Where did that ball go?*

I had invented a new game using a bowl, water and a ball. How clever was that? SWEET! I loved the water and wished I could have done some actual swimming, but the outdoor water bowl just wasn't deep enough.

It took me weeks before I learned that it wasn't a water bowl after all. My neighbor dog Sammy, who witnessed my fence rail debacle in my youth, happened to be out in his yard, and I called him over to take a look at my incredible, outdoor water bowl. My enthusiasm intrigued him, so he lumbered over and put his paws on top of the fence to get a better glimpse of this so called Wonder of the World in the form of a water bowl.

When he locked eyes on the huge water bowl, he glanced at me and laughed so hard that he snorted. "Did you just fall off a Treat Truck? That's no water bowl. That's a baby's swimming pool. This is a whole lot funnier than the fence incident. At least with the fence, you used your head!"

With that, he jumped down and headed back to his house. I could still hear his laughter from my vantage point. It was unmistakable proof that I wasn't the sharpest crayon in the box, and I still lived next door to a comedian.

Anyway, the folks recognized my interest in water which became an obsession with me, and as a treat, they took me for a fun swim at an animal hydrotherapy center. While most of the center's clients suffered from injuries and used the soothing water as a healing experience, fun swims were also offered. I was fascinated by the size of the pool. By this time, I already knew that it wasn't an even larger water bowl than the yellow one in our yard. This one was huge!

Two assistants fitted me with a life jacket and walked me down a ramp into the water. It was warm and soothing. Soon, the ramp ended and I was on my own...actually swimming. SWEET! The assistants waded on either side of me and guided me in the water by the handle on my life jacket. They threw a toy a few feet in front of me, and I was able to retrieve it without difficulty. After a while when they knew I was aquatic friendly, they let loose of the handle and off I went.

*What a glorious feeling!*

My mom circled the exterior of the pool with her camera and marked my swimming debut into digital history. I maneuvered back and forth in the pool while chasing thrown toys…just having a wonderful time. This was the best experience of my life so far; it was even better than the rocket to stardom tour of demonstrations. Applause and praise were definitely worthwhile, but a swim in a huge pool of soothing water was a memory for a lifetime.

*It doesn't get any better than this!*

Eventually, my fun swim time was over, and I had to leave the comfort of the water. I had been swimming vigorously for almost twenty minutes and was happily exhausted. Maybe they'd bring me here again someday. One could always hope.

The next morning, I awoke exhilarated by the water workout from the day before. As I rushed for my morning meal, I noticed that my tail was dragging a bit, and I felt some pain when I attempted to wag it. I wasn't able to wag my tail. What was happening? Did I break my tail? Was that even possible? I was alarmed at the prospect when my folks noticed the lack of tail movement which usually was like a fan on high speed at meal time. I could tell this was serious because they whisked me into the car and never bothered to put me into my crate. I was free in the back seat. Under different circumstances, I might have felt honored but not today. My tail wasn't working, and that wasn't a good sign. What was I without my magnificent tail? Even from the back seat vantage point, I still didn't look out the windows. Instead, I hugged the back seat. POWER TO THE PUP echoed in my head as we went to the animal hospital.

My usual veterinarian was not working that day, so a different doctor examined me. He had a kind face and a gentle touch. While shaking his head, he told my folks that I didn't break my tail but suffered from Limber Tail Syndrome. Apparently, a dog's tail acts as a rudder when in the water, and I had so much activity in the pool the day before that I over did the exercise. He had never seen this syndrome before seeing me. My drooping tail was a milestone for him; and apparently, my tail made his day. Antibiotics and rest would help the situation for me; and in a few days, my tail would be flying high once again.

It happened again when the folks rented a beach house along the coast of North Carolina a few years later. I did the exact same thing to my tail while swimming in the ocean! My dad had me on a long tether, and I was wearing a life jacket; but while the head had fun, the tail suffered that night. This time, Mom and Dad brought the medication in case I sprained my tail again. I still had a rough night, but I sure did have fun in the ocean and wouldn't trade that experience for anything. That ocean was the biggest water bowl I had ever seen! I'm just kidding!

Being in my water world was just the best of times. I lost myself in the soothing water and didn't even give the consequences a thought. I went from backyard baby pool to hydrotherapy pool and eventually, on to the huge ocean.

I had so many experiences, good and bad, throughout the many months spent with my family...the swimming experiences were just a minute portion of my memories. In the weeks to come, I'd take all of those moments with me as I ventured into unknown territory called Puppy College. New and exciting adventures awaited me. While my training during the last twelve months was geared toward this move, the reality of my present situation turning into what might become my future, tickled the hackles on my neck and not in a particularly good way. For one of the few times in my life, I was grateful for the past, stuck in the present and apprehensive of the future...

**11**

# Puppy College

Winter was quickly approaching, and I was already a year old when the family's conversations turned to my going to Puppy College. Was I prepared and would I adjust to the campus life of kennels with regulated training periods? The folks couldn't know, and I certainly wasn't talking. I was in my own little world of adulation from my accumulated fan base. Only time would tell regarding adjustment to new surroundings. My earlier apprehension turned to bravado, although probably false, as I looked forward to my new adventure.

From the beginning of my stay with my family, the folks tried to simulate kennel life with their open concept, wire kennel. I enjoyed my kennel, had a view of everything that went on in the house and could come and go as I pleased. When I ventured into my kennel, I was left entirely alone, had complete privacy and could think about the past, the events of the day or dream of my future. Seriously, I had it made. Why were they so concerned about my adjustment to kennel life in Puppy College? As far as I was concerned, it was just a piece of pup-cake!

Winter came, and I was already used to the snow falling silently from the sky. It was a pretty sight but cold none the less. I partnered with my mom and dad on the remaining various public outings and demonstrations; everything went as planned. While the iciness of the snow sent shivers through my paws, I kept the folks company on their various travels. They always thought of me first and constantly cleaned my paws of debris from the snow and salt that peppered the walks to prevent slipping.

I couldn't ask for better caretakers. However, as the winter months progressed, I detected a sadness that traveled down the leash wherever we went. I would be leaving for Puppy College soon; and while my folks wanted everything good and safe for me in the next part of my journey, they dreaded the loss of my presence and especially my everyday shenanigans. I grew on them like a wart. Those pesky growths are pains in the butt when you have them, but you sure miss them when they're gone. I was their special wart, and they were going to miss me terribly...as I would them.

The week preceding my departure was a week of farewells. My mom and I visited every one of the places that welcomed me during the past year, and everyone said their most heartfelt goodbyes to me. There were a lot of tears that final week, but everyone wanted me to be successful in Puppy College. My neighbor dog, Sammy the Magnificent as I called him, wished me well the day before I left.

As he lumbered over to the fence line, he said "Hey, Bud. (*I don't know why he always called me that. He knew my name, but insisted on calling me Bud*.) Good luck at Puppy College. Don't let the upper class dogs get the best of you. Use your head. That was always your best accessory!"

He was the best...even if he reminded me of all the debacles he witnessed during my youth. Someone had to be the historian, and he definitely fit the bill. The world also had a place for comedians, and he cornered the market on that as well.

We went to church the day before I was to leave, and the priest, who had seen me so many times on Sundays, gave me a special blessing for "those who give service to others." Tears welled in my folk's eyes as the priest blessed me, and I could see that they all just wanted the very best for me. Surprisingly, I wasn't feeling pompous or boastful. I was just grateful for the gracious blessing bestowed upon me from that wonderful priest. Thankfully, he didn't mention the time I tried to drink water from the Holy Water Fountain months ago. Perhaps he had forgotten or had seen that I had grown up a bit and just wished me well.

That night, my mom sat on the floor with me curled on her lap and my head resting on her shoulder. She did this every night from the very first day she brought me to this home. Not only did she sing *You Are My Sunshine* to me, but also added *Let Me Call You Sweetheart* for good luck. While she sang to me, I remembered that cold evening a year ago when she promised that she'd sing to me every night. That was the first of many promises she made to me...and kept.

The next day, my travel bag was packed, and all three of us piled into the car. We were going to Puppy College which was the next chapter in my journey. I jumped into my crate and assumed my regular prone position on the crate's floor. That window phobia still dogged me, and I never knew how to combat it. Once again, I drew on my mantra for courage while riding in the car...POWER TO THE PUP.

This entire window quirk is bizarre. I've done some of the most incredible things and gone to the most unusual places throughout the time with my folks during the past year; yet, I still can't look out the windows of the car. It was such an irrational fear. Nevertheless, it was very real to me. Someday I'll just take the plunge and look out the windows;

but not today.  There was just too much going on for any attempts at bravery on my part.

It took eight hours of driving time to get to Puppy College.  Since we had to register early in the morning, we stayed overnight in a classy motel that not only welcomed me but offered free breakfasts for the guests.  They even had a waffle machine!  Not that it helped me because I was still on dog food, but just knowing that machine was there for public use was exciting to me. This had to be a five star motel!   It was such a treat for me and such a nice prelude to the next chapter in my journey.

In the morning, we went to the Puppy College campus for our designated appointment, and I couldn't figure out why my mom had a few tears in her eyes. This wasn't just a new experience for me. It was Big Dog on Campus time, and I was now ready for the challenge.

We approached the kennel area which I assumed was the dormitory for the matriculating dogs. (*That sounded so collegiate.*)  Surprisingly, the area was a lot larger than I expected.  While concrete floors turned out to be the sleeping area, water and food bowls were strategically placed. Sadly, I noticed there were no granite counter tops or stainless steel appliances. (*I was just kidding about the counter tops and appliances.*)  Overall, the kennel wasn't bad for new digs, and it even had an outdoor patio. One can't get that every day. I was also going to have a kennel mate. Hopefully, he wasn't like the one I traveled with from my California home, but I would soon find out.

My mom slowly took off my cape, collar and leash. After giving me many hugs and kisses, both my mom and dad wished me luck, said that they would miss me terribly, thanked me for being such a wonderful dog, and encouraged me to enter my new digs. I did so willingly since I already saw my roommate who had been outside on the patio. He looked pretty friendly, so I ran to meet him.

He was a sandy colored, Labrador and Golden Retriever mix just like me, but he weighed a whole lot more than I did. His size was a bit imposing. We sniffed each other politely and stayed outside together to investigate the new space. This might turn into a friendship after all.

As my mom and dad were heading towards the front door, I peeked inside and saw that they had tears in their eyes. I made my way over to my kennel mate so they would think that I was okay, but I really wasn't. I was just as sad as they were. A new chapter in my life was beginning; I just didn't know how to do it without them.

The kennel dorm was pretty noisy with the barking and howling around meal time, but it quieted down after meals were served. Tomorrow would be a big day for all of us. We would meet our trainers and be given something called a temperament test. I didn't know what kind of a test that was and had no way to study for it, so I figured I'd ad lib just as I had done many times before in new situations. I also had my POWER TO THE PUP mantra as my safety net.

The first night was a little scary, and vision was limited due to the dim lighting. My kennel mate was pretty cool; and even though I told him my name, he insisted on calling me Dude. *(Who used that word anymore?)* He told me to call him Del. When I asked him about his name or nickname, he just scowled at me...so I just called him Del. As I curled up in what I designated as my corner of the kennel, I lulled myself to sleep with my mantra, and Del's snoring provided the background music.

Bright and early the next day, we were sent outside for a little while and then had our breakfasts. Del was a food gulper; and though I wasn't, I feared that if he finished first, he may just want a sampling of mine. I was trained to eat slowly, but I quickly adopted a faster eating style out of necessity and not out of manners. Down the hatch it went.

Roll call came after meals, and I found out that Del's full name was really Delmond. *Delmond?* No wonder he wanted to be called Del! When his name was called, I didn't even glance at him because if I did, I would have been consumed with laughter. He was bigger than I was, and I had to be careful. Remember, I was a thinker...not a fighter. I wasn't even sure he had a sense of humor. If you had a name like Delmond, would you find it humorous? He must have perfected quite a few self-defense tactics in the dog parks while growing up.

I met my trainer who seemed very nice, and he took me to the training area for the temperament testing. I found out that this type of test was a way of judging a dog's response to certain circumstances. An assistance dog can't react badly if a child might accidently pull the dog's tail, be a bit rough, try to take food from the dog's food bowl or various other situations. What my trainer didn't know was that from the time I was a puppy, my folks would lovingly touch my tail, paws, ears and the scruff of my neck on a daily basis. They would even take some morsels from my food bowl and replace it with something tasty while I was eating. I learned that every time a hand came near my food bowl, something special was coming. The thought of biting the hand that fed me never crossed my mind. Both Del and I passed the temperament testing, but some others didn't do as well. There was a bit more room in the kennel-dorms after that test.

My trainer took me to the training room where dogs of all sizes and ages were working on various skills. I was mesmerized by the talent in that area. These dogs were fantastic. They were opening and closing doors and drawers using rope ties, picking up all sorts of dropped objects, walking slowly next to wheel chairs and just doing incredible things. I was awe struck. That was what I was going to learn to do in my three semesters here, and it was all a bit overwhelming.

My first semester here would be a review of my commands and would determine my proficiency in various areas. While I knew my commands, I didn't always follow through with the correct form. For example, sloppy SITs weren't allowed and STAY meant STAY...not for a little while, but until the FREE command was given. Corrections came swiftly, but rewards came just as fast when the job was done correctly. Proper leash walking was also in the Puppy College Syllabus, and attention definitely centered on that behavior. All in all, it was a lot of work, but I enjoyed it...except for the dreaded leash walking since I seemed to want to get to places first. That was not happening here.

I particularly enjoyed the training area since I worked with a wonderful trainer who helped me with various skills. It gave me a sense of accomplishment when I'd learn a new command, and he always praised me for the good work that I was doing. Seeing the older dogs working diligently at tasks such as picking up dropped objects, using a special technique for emergencies, tapping the Handicapped Panel to open doors, just encouraged me to work harder.

While I really enjoyed the time in training, I dreaded going back to the kennels. My kennel mate was fine, but he was like a drill sergeant. Del told me that he spent a lot of time in his kennel while growing up, and his training was very strict. His attention to detail while executing commands was awe inspiring. If I didn't know better, I'd say he made his right and left turns using a protractor just to get the angles exact. He definitely was a Detail Oriented Dog! I, on the other paw, was a bit more relaxed and was proud that I even knew right from left.

Del and I were similar in some ways, but very different in others. While I preferred my time in the training area or the play area, I wasn't comfortable when I returned to the kennels. All of the dogs spent a lot more time kenneled than working because the trainers worked us hard, and we needed our rest. Del worked hard while in training but enjoyed going to the kennels for his well earned sleep time. That dog had the deepest sleep I had ever seen, and he often slept through major thunderstorms without blinking an eye. While he loved to work, he loved the kennels more. Del believed that sleep was energy for the soul. I just didn't feel that way.

To me, the kennel was a lonely place even though there were many dogs sharing the huge area. I had dogs on each side of my kennel and even a roommate, yet I felt so very alone. I really missed my family; and while I didn't want to disappoint them, I just wasn't adjusting to my surroundings. I still worked well in the training areas, and my trainer was wonderful; but when I was returned to the kennel area, I was miserable. Sadness gave way to my not sleeping and eventually to not being able to keep food down. My mantra wasn't helpful either, and that was a first!

The weeks passed, and I wasn't getting any better. It got to the point where I didn't even want to leave my kennel. I hated feeling like that. Where was that Big Dog on Campus attitude? Where did it go, or was it ever there? Was I so full of myself that I didn't even know the real me? There were no Big Dogs on Campus here. They were just hard working dogs striving to achieve assistance dog status. They wanted to be here and to do what they were in training to do. That was the big difference. In my heart, I knew I didn't have their dedication to the tasks, and that saddened me even more.

Sure, I knew my commands, and I had the public experiences that ordinarily would have prepared most dogs for being successful here. Nevertheless, I had to face the fact that I didn't have the drive that Del had or the perseverance of the older dogs. I wanted the dream, but not being able to adjust to the kennel life was preventing me from making that dream come true.

I wasn't a quitter and wasn't going to give up. Del encouraged me every chance he got, and I gave it all I had to give. While my mind was focused on working hard, my body was fighting me. I was still not eating as much as I should, losing weight, trembling and not eager to leave the sanctuary of the kennel...not even for extra play time in the yard. I had already lost six pounds and just wasn't able to keep food down. Concern registered in the eyes of my trainer as he recognized my difficulty in adjusting. He had me examined by the veterinarian, and it looked like I'd be leaving Puppy College. Apparently, kennel life was just too stressful for me. What would happen to me now, and where would I go?

I didn't go into the training area anymore. Although Del was nice to me, I could see that he was disappointed in me and in my inability to adjust to kennel life. We didn't talk much either. Since we now had nothing in common, there was very little left to say. Our dreams were not intertwined anymore, and our paths changed.

A few days later, my trainer came for me; and while I thought I was being taken to the training area or play yard, I was surprised to be led to the waiting room. With my head down, body trembling and tail tucked, I walked silently into the room...never looking at the people standing in front of me. Then, I heard that soothing voice say, "Kessen, we're here to take you home."

I looked up to see my mom and dad waiting for me. While weak and trembling, I managed a slight wag of my tail. I couldn't believe my eyes. Dreams do come true...I was going home. They weren't disappointed that I couldn't adjust; they wanted me in spite of my not being successful and loved me unconditionally. While I was overwhelmed, I lacked the strength to show it.

My mom led me outside, and the winter wind struck my trembling body with incredible force. My dad lifted me into the canvas crate that had a soft blanket covering the floor area, and my mom wrapped me in her sweatshirt jacket exposing herself to the cold air. She cried for a while on our long trip home, and it wasn't because I was leaving Puppy College. It was my frail appearance that caused her sadness.

Somewhere along that highway, she ran out of tears and so did I. We were all going home together, and that fact alone warmed my heart more than words could ever describe.

However, everything was different now...I was different, and many changes were in store for me...

# 12

# Home at Last

The roads were snow filled and often icy on the way home from Puppy College. Surrounded by the warmth and scent of my mom's sweatshirt as well as the heavy blanket that cushioned the crate's floor, I slept most of the time. We stopped at a few rest stops along the way, but I wasn't really interested in going out in the cold that much. I have that huge bladder, and I definitely could wait for a bit of warmer territory...if that even existed here in the Midwest during winter. My mom gave me water and offered small bits of poached chicken for my tender stomach, but I just wasn't thirsty or hungry. I just wanted to sleep and longed to be back at home where everything was familiar, warm and safe.

It took about eight hours to get home. By the time we got there, we were all exhausted from the emotions of the day. Taking those first steps into the familiar setting was almost like being there for the first time. Because home was so welcoming, I felt free once again. It was a feeling that I missed for weeks. A tremendous weight had been lifted not only from my body but from my spirit as well. Kessen, the Mighty Dog, the Demo Dog or the Big Dog on Campus didn't exist anymore. I was just Kessen...the dog who had to find himself again. Hopefully in time, I would be able to do that with the help of my family. Their unconditional love would give me the strength to be the kind of dog I was meant to be...not the one I pretended to be.

Coming home was more exhausting than I thought was possible. After visiting the dog run, I found a secluded corner of the room and settled into a sound sleep. In my mind, that corner offered safety, but I don't know why I felt that way. Later that evening, my mom once again wrapped her arms around me and began her evening, singing ritual...I don't think I ever enjoyed or appreciated her singing as much as I did that first, memorable night home from Puppy College. It was undeniable proof that this home was where I belonged.

After I found a safe corner for the night, I heard my mom tell my dad that if she hadn't seen the black spot on my side, the one my sister Kelyn called my "doorbell", she would not have recognized me at the kennels. Seeing tears in their eyes was the last thing I saw before falling into a deep sleep.

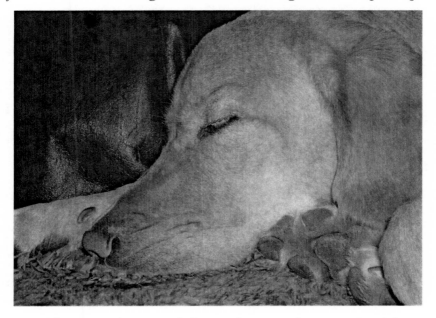

The next day, my folks took me to be examined by my favorite veterinarian. I was diagnosed with colitis, prescribed medication, put on special food and allowed to get as much rest as needed. That lasted about six weeks, yet I continued to sleep in various corners of the house. At first, it baffled my folks since they had a comfortable bed for me in my kennel, but they just decided to let me work it out in my own time.

It was difficult to deal with my lack of success in Puppy College since I had been such a pompous pup. My plan was to be a Big Dog on Campus...what a joke that was. Everyone there, including Del, was wonderful to me, and Puppy College was a great place. As it turned out, it just wasn't for me, and that was extremely disappointing. Prior to going there, I had thought of myself as a bit of a big shot...a dog who was destined from birth for service. Humility was never one of my attributes...until now

Eventually, I came to terms with the disappointment in myself and was even given the choice of either sleeping in my open concept kennel in the bedroom or sleeping on the bed at night. While in training, I was never allowed on the furniture, so this was a big opportunity for me. I didn't choose it right away. I spent a few days in the security of my kennel; but then after a few days, I chose the bed and have stayed there ever since. It's a whole lot more comfortable than the kennel floor...even with a blanket in it. I still slept in corners during the day, and I still won't look out the car windows either. These are definitely strange behaviors. The mind is such a mysterious mechanism.

When I wasn't sleeping, I spent a lot of time looking out the bay window in our family room. I'd watch the neighborhood kids as they waited for the school bus or the joggers getting in their daily exercise. I remembered that when I was very young, I'd enjoy doing the exact same thing. Since I was too small to reach the window, my mom put my toy box under the window, and I'd jump up on the box for a front seat.

*Best seat in the house.*

Sometimes I'd even rest there with a very special toy in my mouth...just watching the world go by. Mom and Dad called me their Box Boy!

*Box Boy was a great nickname!*

Remembering those happy moments and reliving them once again helped me on my road to recovery. Being able to look out the window without standing on a toy box was a bonus!

I'd been home about six weeks when I started to feel better both physically and mentally. I'd gained some weight, lost the frail appearance and was more active during the day. Sleeping so much had its benefits. I now believed in Del's philosophy that sleep was energy for the soul, but I'd have to add that it was definitely energy for the body as well. I had to snap out of my mood, but that was easier said than done. I had a pity party going on for much too long, and it wasn't much of a party with me as the one and only guest. That realization gave me the encouragement I needed, and I was determined to spring back into action.

During those icy and snowy winter months, my mom kept up with my commands in the house. She thought it would be good mental stimulation for me. For a while, I just went through the motions knowing it was pleasing to her to see me working again. Soon I was demonstrating some crisp SITs, drop to the floor DOWNs and lengthy STAYs. The K-Man was making a comeback. Once the weather changed, snow was replaced by signs of early spring, gray skies turned to blue and the sun actually shined. Daily walks outside became my routine; and even my leash behavior improved, but it wasn't consistently top notch. Once again, I had pep in my paws, and each day held the promise of fun and adventure.

Sleeping in corners wasn't the only baggage I brought home from Puppy College; this new one involved walking in the neighborhood. Seeing a dog coming towards me, even a block away, caused a most undesirable change in both my body language and my behavior. I'd bark and carry on in the most bizarre way. This was shameful behavior on my part, yet it only happened while walking in the neighborhood. I went to classes, to pet stores, to the groomer and other places where dogs congregated, and I never reacted negatively. On the other paw, seeing a dog in the distance while walking in the neighborhood brought out the dog distraction in me. Yet, I loved going for walks. My mom said walking me was like walking a time bomb through a mine field. While it was a rather harsh assessment, it was nonetheless very accurate. Since I was considerably stronger now, my mom might not be able to control me during those unpleasant moments. So, my dad took over as Captain of the Bomb Squad and handled the daily walks.

I had hit the trifecta of behavioral issues: I refused to look out of the car windows, repeatedly slept in corners, and was fairly unpredictable on walks. I was quite the catch! While some folks might have just given up and let me play around in the yard for exercise, my folks were determined to redirect this misconduct on my part; the daily walks continued.

Thinking that I was a perfect candidate for a private lesson, my folks took me to my former obedience training facility. The instructor brought her dogs to serve as distractions. Her plan was to walk them by me from a distance and then gradually move closer to elicit my adverse reaction. Then, attempts at systematic desensitization would be made to extinguish the negative behavior. She walked each dog back and forth; then she resorted to running with them. I didn't react in any way. It appeared that my crazed canine alter ego slept during the exercise. Since I showed no reaction other than to catch a few winks during the exercise, they took me outside to repeat the process. Once again, neither of the dogs bothered me as they walked or ran by. It wasn't that I was uncooperative; their actions just didn't conjure up the crazed canine that surfaced during walks in the neighborhood. Ultimately, it was a costly endeavor for my mom and dad.

Nevertheless, giving up wasn't in their vocabulary as far as I was concerned. My dad then took me to a class for rowdy dogs. Still, I showed no undesirable response. It only happened in neighborhood walks. Truth be told, I didn't even know why the lovable me turned into that crazed canine. My dad, the Captain of the Bomb Squad, took me for walks very early in the morning when opportunities for my split personality to emerge were limited. Why couldn't I recognize what caused this behavior in me, and why couldn't I control it? Nevertheless, my dad persevered despite all odds; perhaps he was working towards a change in status from Captain to General of the Bomb Squad!

Before I went off to Puppy College, having dogs stay at our house for a few days wasn't unusual. I remembered the adventures I had with a good friend named Turin.

*Sleepover buddy.*

He had been raised by my folks for potential service a year before I came to their home. He and I had lots of fun together, and remembering those fun times made me very happy. Pace was another handsome, black Labrador Retriever who stayed with us for a weekend. While on the way to our house, he devoured an entire bag of donut holes that were on the back seat of the car. Some of the paper bag was eaten as well. The dog run was treated to a new experience that weekend, but Pace's breath sure smelled great. It just proves that every cloud has a silver lining. Other dogs stayed at our house as well over the years, and having some canine companionship was an added bonus to having my family.

However, when I first returned from Puppy College, my folks stopped puppy sitting for a while. They wanted me to feel better before bringing another dog into the house. Now, I believed I was ready for some canine companionship. The prospect of enjoying the company of another dog in the house promised adventures of enormous proportions as well as a little mischief as a bonus. Those imaginary yard villains and foes of my puppyhood days weren't going to cut it anymore. I was ready for some real excitement of the four legged variety. Once again, K-Man was back on his paws and ready to rock and roll.

For the next few months, dogs often stayed with us, and I was the perfect host for the visiting canines. I never displayed my dog distraction issue while in the house or yard. It was just a strange behavior that I apparently reserved for daily walks in the neighborhood with my dad, the Captain, now close to becoming the General.

For the first time in a few months, I felt good about myself. The colitis was gone, and I was gradually weaned back on my regular dog food. It wasn't as tasty as the special food, but one can't have it all. Aside from the car window phobia, the sleeping in corners and dog distraction baggage, I was my happy go lucky self. I enjoyed the company of adults as well as dogs visiting our house and I was, generally, well behaved. Since I wasn't in training anymore, I could even sleep on the couch!

*I'm now a couch potato.*

Life took on a somewhat normal pace; and as life would have it, lulled me into a false sense of security at the same time. I felt that I was truly home at last. However, nothing ever stays the same. A major change was coming my way, and it arrived in the form of a most unexpected package...

# 13

# Snore Baby Snore

Unlike people, dogs use their capacity for sniffing to update their daily information. It is one of my morning rituals and is comparable to people reading the newspaper. While standing on the deck early one morning, I sniffed the air for the latest comings and goings in the neighborhood. I found out that rabbits lived under the next door neighbor's deck, a skunk had crossed the property behind us some time during the night, the chipmunks infested the territory near the tomato plants in our yard, and our neighbor just got another puppy. His first dog was quite the neighborhood gossip and kept us all informed about the tawdry side of our canine community. That dog had a real grasp of information and spent a lot of time sniffing up the news and barking it to the neighborhood.

Today, I wasn't given the same leeway in terms of sniffing time, and my information was a bit limited. Apparently, the folks were going to some airport to pick up a special package, and my Auntie Deb and Auntie Brenda were coming to spend the day with me. They are good friends who stay at our house when my folks travel without me. My Aunties are like family to me and keep me out of trouble. It is a thankless job, but someone has to do it. I have lots of fun with them, and my Auntie Deb even plays her own version of the "sniffing game" with me. She gets down on the carpet and spins around while I try to sniff her face. Words can't describe the fun and excitement of that game. I knew that we would play it sometime after my folks left. I really enjoy the time they spend with me, and I believe they enjoy my antics as well.

Anyway, the sitters arrived, and my mom and my dad were just about ready to leave for the airport in Milwaukee, Wisconsin. It would take a few hours to get there, and they were getting an early start. That seemed like a long way to go to pick up a package, but people are sometimes difficult to understand. They also told me that the package was going to be a great surprise for me and was something that I would definitely enjoy.

Now, why would they tell me they were getting a surprise for me and then not tell me what it was? That just didn't seem right. I assumed my most successful begging position, yet they weren't going to ruin the surprise. They just left me to dwell on what they said and to spend the day anticipating what sort of package was yet to come. *I thought dogs weren't supposed to be teased!* However, my attention was quickly diverted from the surprise package intrigue by the announcement of the "sniffing game." I was "in it to win it," and thoughts of the surprise package were forgotten.

While the folks were on their pilgrimage for the package, I noticed that the house looked a bit different. There were gates separating the kitchen, dining room and family room from the rest of the house. My very first open concept kennel was positioned in the corner of the kitchen as well as a set of food and water bowls in a slightly elevated stand. They were nothing like the ones I had. My bowls were much higher off the floor so I didn't have to bend to eat or drink. My old toy box was also positioned by the bay window. What was going on? It looked familiar and reminiscent of the arrangement when I first arrived in this household a few years ago.

When I heard the car pull into the driveway, I rushed to my assigned position for appropriate greetings. Waiting anxiously for the door to open, excitement over the impending surprise package surged through my body. As the door slowly opened, I immediately saw the package that my mom held in her arms. Time stood still for me, and I do believe that my heart skipped a beat.

Mom carried the most beautiful puppy that I had ever seen. The new arrival was very young and quite petite, perhaps only ten pounds soaking wet. Her flaxen coat was smooth as silk, and velvet-textured ears framed her angelic face. A nose, as black as coal, drew attention to her eyes which were her most striking feature. They were the color of rich, dark chocolate...the good stuff, not the waxy kind. Everything about her was delicate. I was instantly smitten and imagined what a beauty she'd be a year from now when she was older and of courting age. My mom, seeing how excited I was to meet her, introduced her as Brighton or Brightie for short. She was to be treated as my new, little sister.

*She's my sister?*

*Sister*? Tell me you didn't say sister! Any dreams of future romance went out the window with that announcement. Apparently, my new job was that of big brother to this tiny tyke. Before my mom's announcement, Brightie was destined to be the love of my life. Now, she was just a tiny tyke. She was quite the surprise package; more like the-joke-is-on-me kind of package! Life is just not fair.

*Welcome to your new home.*

So Brightie came into my life as my so-called little sister. She walked gracefully towards me on those dainty paws. When she looked up at me with those dazzling eyes, a protective feeling rushed over me. This elfin puppy needed me to watch over her, and I was up for the task. Our tentative sniffing served as an appropriate greeting followed by a trip to the dog run. When we returned, she walked right into her kennel without any encouragement whatsoever and immediately fell asleep. That went much better than my first venture into the kennel. After seeing this, I believed that watching over Brightie was going to be quite an easy job.

My mom then explained that Brightie came from California, was a mix of Labrador Retriever and Golden Retriever just like me, but more Lab than Golden judging from her shorter coat and body shape. She was an assistance pup in training…just as I was almost two years ago. Brightie would follow the same training schedule that I used, and eventually she too would go to Puppy College. However, she had an additional goal. Brightie was identified as a possible breeder; so her physical characteristics, temperament and training goals were each very important for her to reach. I supposed that being considered for both an assistance dog and a breeder qualified as having a double major in Puppy College. Brightie sure was a special puppy.

*She looks special, doesn't she?*

Remembering how exhausted I was when I first traveled from California, I knew that Brightie had to be tired and miserable about leaving her family. Thoughts of my birth mother's sad eyes as the car carrying her family left the driveway momentarily brought me back to that place and time years ago. I hadn't thought of that for a while, and that memory made me realize how terrible Brightie must feel right now. We would all work together to make her feel loved and at home here with us. That was my promise to her as she slept, and it was a promise that I was determined to keep. A puppy that small couldn't possibly take care of herself. That was the job of a big brother, and I fit the bill.

Thinking that a familiar face and scent would put her at ease, I settled into a place next to her kennel in case she woke up and was frightened in her new surroundings. I was taking my big brother role seriously; and while feeling quite good about myself, I drifted off to sleep.

About three hours later, I was awakened by the most ear shattering screech I had ever heard. Concern for temporary deafness momentarily filled my mind. When I heard the shrieking again, I knew that at least my hearing was intact. What form of creature made sounds like that? Certainly it was not one of this world. Out of concern for Brightie's well being, I looked into her kennel to make sure she was safe. Imagine my shock and surprise when I realized that not only was Brightie awake, but the ear shattering sounds came from her tiny throat. Was a megaphone hidden in her mouth? If so, how did it get there? The wailing continued, and my mom and dad covered her kennel with a sheet to stop the sounds or at least muffle them. That simplistic approach may have worked on me years ago, but it wasn't working now.

Brightie's volume control was on high, and she demonstrated vocal stamina for much of the night. I was sure that we'd all be deaf by morning. While pulling the ends of the sheet into her kennel through the wire openings, she took time for a few breaths in between screeching and howling. I'll say this...she was definitely determined and capable of multi-tasking at a very early age. My wishful thinking of my role as big brother was quickly altered. Brightie didn't need protection; I did. Perhaps, we all did. The honeymoon was undeniably over.

Morning came, and we were all bleary eyed from lack of sleep...except for Brightie. She was tossing her body around the kennel in an attempt to escape while adding a new dimension to her vocal tones. That girl could screech! Anyway, my mom waited until Brightie settled down before letting her out of the kennel and when she did, Brightie just ran to the door and out into the dog run. Afterwards, she ran back into the house, ate a nice meal and went back into her kennel to rest.

My mom told me that in a little while, I could spend time playing with her. After the all night concert, that was the last thing I wanted to do. However, looking at Brightie quietly sleeping in her kennel made the events of the night seem a bit exaggerated. Perhaps, it wasn't as dreadful as I remembered. So I was going to start fresh this morning with a new attitude toward her.

When Brightie woke up, my mom let her out and toys were positioned all over the floor for play time. She enthusiastically bounded out of her wire enclosure and looked at the array of toys. However, she decided to spend some time with me instead. I was flattered that she chose me over a fluffy duck that quacked when scrunched or the hedgehog that jumped around if pushed. Flopping down on the floor next to her so she could easily say a polite good morning, I was caught off guard by her sudden launch toward my face. She grabbed onto my muzzle and squeezed. This little one not only had razor sharp teeth, but hidden strength in that tiny jaw of hers. What I anticipated as being a well-mannered, morning greeting turned into a full frontal attack. I tried shaking her off, but she just wouldn't let go. Pain surged through my face. If she had been a male puppy, I might have responded differently, but Linus taught me never to bite a lady. Instead, I just stopped moving and stood perfectly still. This change in motion surprised her; and when she released her grip on my face, I ran from the room. I wasn't proud of my hasty retreat, but my face is my moneymaker!

All of this happened in the blink of an eye. Although from my perspective, it lasted quite a bit longer since I was on the other end of Brightie's vice-like grip. My mom raced over as quickly as she could, but the attack was over by the time she reached the scene. Mom checked my face to make sure I wasn't bleeding and sent me on my way. That's it? There's no sympathy offered for the unprovoked attack? Apparently, sympathy was not warranted.

I was safely positioned on the other side of the fence while Brightie settled down with her toys. Not even a look of apology came from that angelic face. Instead, she looked a bit smug. She definitely wasn't all that beautiful to me anymore. Some kind of evil lurked behind those gorgeous eyes. Whatever it was seemed to have a special liking for my face. I stayed out of her way for a few days and hid within the security of my corners. Those are considered my safe places and off limits to everyone. Playing with her would not be an option as long as I stayed within the confines of my corners.

The next week, my folks took Brightie for a play date with her brother Bart. He lived with another family nearby.

Someone should have warned him about Brightie's facial attacks. I would have issued the danger alert, but not only were my paws too big to use the phone's key pad, I wasn't even allowed to use the phone. Sorry, Bart. You're on your own.

Off they went for the play date; but before I had a decent amount of peaceful sleep, they returned. Judging from my mom's unhappy expression, the experience did not go well. As it happened, a fight broke out between the siblings early in play and was instigated by the one and only, Brightie the Bad. In order to end the altercation, splashing water on her was necessary to loosen Brightie's vice-like grip. It wasn't just puppy stuff either. Puppies do play rough, but when an expression of pain is given, the play is supposed to end much like the bell ringing at the end of a boxing match. Opponents stop the action and go to their separate corners. Brightie obviously was not at all inclined to follow rules of good sportsmanship.

Brightie's actions went beyond the norm for puppy antics, and she did not limit her attacks to the canine world. My folks had also been the victims of her unprovoked attacks. The typical sound of the word "ouch" held no meaning for this elfin dynamo and in no way deterred her from her hostile behavior. She was an equal opportunity aggressor, and no one was safe.

Most folks would send a puppy like that back but not mine. Just as they persevered with my foolishness in terms of neighborhood walking, they did the same for Brightie and her behavior. There had to be a reason for such negative conduct. No puppy starts out in life like this without something causing it. Mom thought that perhaps a trainer might have some insights into how to successfully work with Brightie. A trainer? I suggested looking for an exorcist. Someone needed to check that blonde bombshell for 666 hidden somewhere on her body.

Doing some research of the litter's background, my mom found out that Brightie was the first born, the smallest and was picked on by her litter mates on a daily basis. Considering the fight or flight response, Brightie chose to fight rather than flee and consequently became a bully. That might explain her need to be the aggressor.

My mom also checked out the physical component. Perhaps Brightie suffered from some sort of infection that made her uncomfortable and contributed to her less than friendly behavior. Off they went to the veterinarian and sure enough, Brightie had a severe urinary infection and was prescribed medication.

It took about three months for her system to rid itself of infection. In the meantime, my mom worked with her in terms of her behavior. Sometimes Mom even wore leather gloves as defense against those razor sharp, puppy teeth. When Brightie became aggressive, my mom said nothing but left the room. Being alone was more of a punishment for Brightie than any form of reprimand. She was also unresponsive to forcefully issued commands. Instead, a soft, monotone was used in training. Trying to find the right training technique took time and patience since Brightie's learning style didn't fit any of the textbook's techniques. Not even my mom's Tool Box of Tricks held any usable tactics. After scouring the bookstore shelves, the internet and the use of trial-and-error, my mom eventually came up with the combination of techniques that worked with Brightie. Now, her training began in earnest.

While Brightie's training progressed, her socialization skills were sorely lacking, and the condition of my face was proof of that. I did my best to bob and weave to avoid her launches, but the little tyke's size worked in her favor. My size and weight, on the other hand, worked against me. That dynamo had speed. I was having quite the difficult time. Since I never retaliated, it was a losing battle for me from the get go. She knew that her big brother was not going to fight back, so it was a win-win situation for her. Socialization just wasn't her thing. She reminded me a little bit of myself at her age, but I was certainly nowhere near as extreme.

The thought of being Brightie's very own chew toy for the year she'd live here sent shivers down my spine, especially since her new teeth would only get bigger and her jaw a lot stronger. That didn't seem possible, but the nature of maturity and growth was proof of that eventuality. I was given a brief reprieve when she lost her baby teeth, but that didn't last long. Those new, pearly whites were popping up fast in that mouth of hers. Being her big brother was not easy; in fact, it was downright painful at times.

My mom recognized Brightie's shortcomings in terms of socialization as well as the beating I was taking on a regular basis. Her special announcement made my spirits soar and brought hope to my situation. According to my mom, it was time to bring in the Big Guns!

That meant only one thing...Linus was coming to spend a few days with us. Yippee! The Big Gun was on his way, and I couldn't wait for the show to begin. This time, I'd observe his Three Step Action Plan from the audience side of his mouth...the sidelines of safety. The sheriff was coming to town, and I was filled with anticipation over the prospect of seeing Brightie match wits with him. This was going to be a huge event. With any luck, it would last a few days. What greater reward than payback from afar. Bravery was never one of my strengths.

Linus spent a week with us, and seeing him spring into action the first time she launched her tiny body at him was a sight etched in my mind forever.

*Linus works his magic.*

He never touched her, but his perfected use of the Three Step Action Plan gave her an entirely new perspective regarding the purpose of teeth and their relationship to appropriate canine behavior. His masterful use of the lip quiver, the low growl and the muffled snap was poetry in motion. The little Diva had met her match.

At first, he worked entirely with Brightie. In all honesty, she responded much faster to his Three Step Action Plan than I did when I was a pup. While I can't accept that she is smarter, I might concede that her decision making skills were more advanced than mine at that age. Did females mature earlier than males? My developmental history wasn't exactly the best data to dispute that possibility.

Nevertheless, it was my turn to assume my proper position in the pack, and Linus assured me that he'd watch my back or rather my face. Within a few days, the pack order was established. Linus was always first; I was next and then, Brightie. That protocol was followed in everything we did from going out to the dog run, eating or playing with toys. Brightie and I did some supervised jaw sparring and air snapping, but she never chomped on my face again.

*We're friends now.*

Linus had another successful socialization notch added to his collar and saved me from a year's worth of puncture wounds to my face. Linus rocked!

While Brightie adjusted well to the canine world, she played nicely with me and with the puppies in Puppy Kindergarten. However, her trust issues with the folks continued. Every night after my turn, Mom did her singing ritual with Brightie; and night after night, Brightie struggled. During training, she never launched herself at the folks anymore, but she never approached them for comfort either. She just remained aloof. My mom, patient as ever, continued to be kind to her, remained consistent with expectations and worked toward helping Brightie feel safe.

One night when Brightie was about five months old, my mom was working with her in the kitchen. While seated on the floor, my mom prepared for the nightly singing ritual. With the expectation of a struggle, my mom gently lifted Brightie into her lap, and the most fascinating thing happened. Rather than resist, Brightie curled up in her lap, laid her head on my mother's shoulder and sighed contentedly. The struggle was over, and Brightie was on the road to trusting people. Seeing that made me love that little tyke once again.

*Brightie officially joined the family.*

That night, Brightie quietly entered her kennel. For the first time, there weren't any intermittent screeching or howling sounds. Instead, a strange guttural sound came from her enclosure. As I peeked in, I saw her elfin body curled around her cuddly duck toy, and the bizarre sound was the sound of her snoring. All of the intense volume of her past screeching was now projected in her snoring. That girl could snore with the best of them! Looking at her sleeping body and knowing that she finally found some peace in her life, all I could say was, "Snore Baby Snore." It was so much better than the howling, but realistically, just as scary in terms of volume and intensity.

We had a lot to look forward to in the year ahead of us. With the help of Linus, events would be relatively pain free. My face was intact, and I once again safely assumed the role of big brother. While having a little sister was fun, I missed my sister Kelyn very much. I thought of her often and wondered what had become of her. I wished we had said goodbye to each other on that day we were separated or kept in touch in some way. There were other wishes from past experiences that turned into regrets, but I guess that happens in life. What I was to find out later was that wishes, unlike regrets, do sometimes come true...

# 14

## An Unforgettable Reunion

Weeks passed, and summer finally arrived. The blue skies, while not as blue as those in California, reminded me of my early puppy days. Memories flooded my brain of those early days, lying on my back in my special meadow while looking at the cloudless skies with my sister Kelyn. Back then, we were living the good life of fun and frolic. That feeling of well-being still lingered in the recesses of my mind as well as in a special place in my heart. I'd draw upon that feeling of comfort for refuge in times of sadness, but in all honesty, I experienced very little unhappiness. I had the best life with my wonderful, caring family...even including my so-called little, sister Brightie.

Brightie and I had very different schedules that summer. I spent most of my days following the sun from place to place in the house and sleeping contentedly in its warmth. Time was also spent sniffing for information on the deck, rolling around in the grass or chasing butterflies. On the other paw, Brightie had begun her public outing phase, and she would go on some field trip each day with my mom and dad. That offered me the peace and quiet of an empty house. Life was good.

Brightie and I were different in so many ways. I'll admit that I was a bit envious of Brightie's daily public outing schedule. While I was in training, public appearances were such special events for me. Thinking back on my public outing phase, I couldn't help but remember how thrilled I was to visit various places and how my imagination would soar while wearing my cape. Not only was it a symbol of pride, but the cape became a magical cloak that transformed me into a super action hero. I became Kessen, the Mighty Dog...star of restaurants, malls, churches, classrooms and various indoor and outdoor places. Granted, all that changed when I went to Puppy College and I realized how silly I was. Prior to that, I had a good time...if only in my own mind!

On the other paw, Brightie had quite a different view of public appearances. While she enjoyed going out every day, she was not at all impressed with wearing her cape. She was quite petite and still had to do some growing for it to fit correctly. According to her, it did nothing for her figure, and the color didn't enhance her eyes. The cape held no magic for her.

*I thought she looked good in it.*

Being in public didn't have the same excitement for Brightie as it did for me. While she enjoyed the greetings and the attention, it wasn't something that energized her like it did me. She was out to do a job, and she'd do it. Applause was nothing she wanted or needed. We were so very different.

Since we couldn't run around the house, we spent time in the evening chasing after each other in the yard. We did a little jaw sparring and air snapping just to keep it lively. My dad always kept the hose handy in case we got too rough. I think he only used it once, and that was to get our attention. When he did that, we would jump at the spray of water coming from the hose. Somehow Brightie was able to accomplish that without getting wet. I never understood how she was able to do that since I always got soaked. It must be a female thing.

I tried to fool Brightie into believing that the round, yellow container in the yard was a huge, water bowl, but she already knew it was a baby's pool. How come she knew that, and I didn't when I first saw it? There just might be something to the idea that the female mind might mature faster than the male mind. I'll have to evaluate the data.

Anyway, our days just flew by. Toward the end of the summer, the folks mentioned that we were taking an important field trip to North Carolina for a few weeks and there would be a special surprise for me when we got there. Oh, no...another pilgrimage, and this time we were all going. Hopefully, it wasn't for another so-called sister. My face hasn't healed yet.

This time, I played it smart. I pretended that I didn't even want to know what it was. That mystery surprise would be there when we got to North Carolina, and I was not even going to give it a second thought. Brightie said that she knew what it was since she heard my mom and dad talking about it while in the restaurant. Brightie heard everything from under the table and thought she'd use the secret as some sort of leverage towards favors. Well, it wouldn't work this time. I was not taking the bait.

Brightie asked for favors all of the time. I called her the Get Me-Gimme Girl. It was always get me a toy or gimme the bone...the one that's actually in my mouth. You get me this and gimme that. Next, she'd flutter those curly eyelashes surrounding her gorgeous, mocha colored eyes in hopes of enticing me into being her Go-Get Dog.

*I won't be fooled by her feminine wiles.*

It was not going to happen this time. Sure, I did things for her at first but not anymore. I was on to her feminine wiles and refused to be charmed by her into doing her bidding just to find out what surprise awaited me. I was just not interested, and I meant it.

The day to leave for North Carolina finally arrived. Brightie's canvas crate was in the back section of Sparky 2 along with the luggage, and I was in the back seat wearing a travel harness. We were all set to go. Brightie continued to laugh at me because I still wouldn't look out of the car windows. She predicted that one day I would overcome the fear because it would help someone else. She was talking nonsense again so it went in one floppy ear and out the other one. She was my travel guide and described all of the sights as we rolled along. I had to use my imagination to conjure up the images, but I was good at that. My vivid imagination is one of my strengths.

My dad drove for about eight hours with a few stops in between for washroom breaks, and we finally arrived at the motel. It was a nice place and was dog friendly. A few people stopped to pet us, but we didn't hang around the lobby. Instead, we all went to the room and settled in for the night. For some reason, everyone was pretty tired.

The next morning after we all had breakfast, we were once again on the highway getting closer and closer to my surprise. I'll admit, I was getting a bit excited; but I didn't dare let Brightie know. She had already tempted me numerous times with inklings of what was to come; I wasn't giving into her charms. I'd probably end up being her servant for the rest of the year if I gave in and asked her to tell me about the surprise. Her information didn't come cheap!

I slept most of the day and only woke up for rest stops. Since I wasn't looking out the windows, the only thing left to do was sleep. Brightie talked about the sights, the weather, the trees, the cars and just about everything that was either in front of us or behind us. That girl only stopped to take a breath or a short nap. Girl, give it a rest!

About eight hours into the journey on this day, my mom made the announcement from the front seat that we just crossed into North Carolina and would be reaching the motel in a little while. We were staying at two motels on this trip. This must be very special. Brightie had this know-it-all expression on her face because she was in on the surprise, but I had waited two days already...I could wait a bit longer.

The folks checked into the motel, unloaded the luggage, had a brief dinner, fed us and let us rest for a little while after eating. Dogs with big chests like Labs and Goldens have to rest after eating to avoid bloat which is a serious stomach condition that is often fatal. An hour later, they took us for a short walk to get the traveling kinks out of our joints, and we were then ushered back into the car. This wasn't a trip; it was a pilgrimage just to get to the surprise, and it was taking forever. Maybe the surprise was the pilgrimage, or perhaps there was no surprise. After all, I had been teased in the past. Wouldn't that be something if that were true? I knew my folks wouldn't do that to me. Brightie might but not my mom or dad. However, the expression on Brightie's face made me believe that there was actually something special waiting for me, and she really looked happy for me. That fact alone made me a bit suspicious.

About fifteen minutes later, we pulled into a driveway and were greeted by a very attractive woman with smiling eyes and yet another handsome man like my dad. What a stunning couple this woman and man made. Was meeting them the surprise? Who were they?

Judging from the adults' conversation, this was the first time they had all met face to face, but apparently the woman and my mom had communicated on the internet for well over a year. They talked as if they knew each other well. Brightie and I were taken out of the car, introduced and were expected to be on our best behavior…at least I was. Brightie's foolishness was accepted as part of her being young. Such double standards are allowed in the canine world.

They were a most gracious couple…delighted over Brightie's petite glamour and thought that my slender build and handsome face made me quite the dog's dog. Knowing how much I enjoyed being adored, I was thrilled beyond expectations. If this was the surprise, it was a good one. I liked these people.

Yet, the woman couldn't take her eyes off me (*It's not the first time that happened. After all, I am an all species chick magnet.*) and she commented how much her dog and I looked alike…except for the difference in length of coat. I really wasn't sure why that mattered since those of us who were mixed breeds often shared the same physical characteristics. She took my leash and led me into her house. My mom, my dad and the woman's husband followed behind with Brightie.

We were met by a cacophony of sounds. It sounded like a pack of dogs running around the house; and believe it or not, that's exactly what it was! They were led by a gorgeous, long haired, honey colored Golden Retriever, possibly a mix like me. I couldn't be sure because I only caught a glimpse of her as she literally raced by me on the first pass. As the pack flew by, I saw a Gordon Setter followed by a tiny Cavalier King Charles Spaniel/Dachshund mix just a bit ahead of an English Golden Retriever. This was like the United Nations of the dog world. They were having a glorious time and didn't even notice our presence in the doorway. By the second time around, their speed had accelerated and as the Golden raced past me, she hesitated long enough to catch a fly mid-air. The only dog I ever knew who could do that was my sister Kelyn.

I wistfully whispered her name as she passed me the third time, and all of a sudden, she skidded to a stop...the other dogs piling up on each other behind her. Turning to me and studying my face, she had a spark of recognition in those dark eyes of hers. She tentatively sauntered over, scrutinized my appearance and paid particular attention to my side. She was looking for signs of the black spot in my coat that she aptly nicknamed my "doorbell" when we were pups. Upon seeing it, tears welled in her eyes as they did in mine...and in everyone else's who were watching us. There was not a dry eye in the room. Miracle of miracles...this gorgeous dog was my beloved sister Kelyn...older and much prettier than I would ever have imagined.

*Kelyn is so beautiful.*

All of my fears and concerns for her melted away as we sniffed and greeted each other...each of us hoping this was not a dream.

With those formalities out of the way, we raced after each other in the yard, tumbled around, jaw sparred and air snapped just as we did in our special meadow long ago. This reunion was the very best surprise I had ever experienced. Nothing would ever top this.

*Reunited and it feels so good.*

The other dogs joined in, and after we ran around until exhaustion set in, we all decided to rest a bit and get to know each other. I made sure to introduce my other sister Brightie first. After all, she had kept that secret, and it was really a big one at that. Kelyn then introduced her pack members.

Sidney, the Gordon Setter, was very dignified looking with his coal-like coat and rust colored fringe. He was the dignitary of the group although he did suffer periodically from separation anxiety. Beppe, a Cavalier King Charles Spaniel/ Dachshund mix, was left with Kelyn's mom to watch while the original owners got settled in their new home in another state. That was fifteen years ago, and they still haven't returned to claim him. Shame on them, but that was their loss and not Beppe's! The third member of Kelyn's pack was a dazzling English Golden Retriever named Carly. She was quite spectacular with her flowing white coat and tan ears framing one of the kindest faces I had ever seen. Carly suffered from a medical condition that was diagnosed very early in her life. Rather than give her up, her mom devised a specialized rehabilitation plan. Today, Carly is happy, healthy and, might I add, quite the looker.

*Where's Beppe?*

All of us got along so well. In between running around the yard, we shared stories of our puppyhood experiences. When our antics got rough, Sidney, whose anxiety prevented him from joining in, positioned himself on the sidelines and enjoyed watching us make fools of each other from a safe distance.

*Carly, Brightie, Kelyn and I smile for the camera.*

Later, when we were all exhausted from the rigorous play, Kelyn told me about her coming to Charlotte, North Carolina when we were separated that day. Her kind mom and dad, who I now call Auntie Jan and Uncle Don, trained her just as my mom and dad had done with me. In addition to raising potential assistance dogs and rescuing dogs in need,

179

Auntie Jan was actually a Certified Trainer. Now, that's very impressive. Our moms met through the assistance dog organization's online communication system. Individuals who raise puppies for potential service exchange information with the other families of same littermates. It seemed that they communicated with each other about us from the time we arrived from California.

Apparently, Kelyn and I shared some of the same characteristics while growing up. Our shared sensitivity led to both of us being released from Puppy College, but Auntie Jan adopted Kelyn just as my mom adopted me. We live in such a small world.

This was a most unforgettable reunion, and one that I'll cherish forever. I love my mom and dad, but this put my love for them over the top. They somehow knew how much I needed to re-connect with Kelyn, and they made it happen. How could I ever repay them for this act of kindness? In a world where things sometimes go wrong more than right, I realized that dreams occasionally do come true.

I was overwhelmed by the events of the day, and that part of my mind that dwelt on my sister's whereabouts was now at peace. She was safe, loved and enjoying her life. There would never be a surprise as great as this...never, ever again. However, traveling into South Carolina the next day, I found myself wondering if what happened next was a close second.  As they say, never say never...

## Backyard Bonanza

Following the events of the unexpected reunion, we all traveled back to the motel to rest for the night. We had a big day ahead of us tomorrow. While I didn't quite know what that meant, I was ready for anything. The events of the day left me drained of emotion and so deeply relieved that my sister Kelyn was safe and living the good life. I was now at peace with regards to her safety and well-being.

Brightie and I settled in for the night and exchanged a few thoughts about our family situations. We each shared different beginnings. Whatever our differences, we were all still loved and had what we called "created families" instead of our biological ones. These wonderful people picked us to love as their own, and we needed to acknowledge that commitment.

I slept soundly for probably the first time since my separation from my biological family. I awoke rested and ready for the events of the day. Seeing Kelyn and her family again was really going to be fun, and I couldn't wait to get there. I was really anticipating that meeting.

When we got there, Brightie and I were let loose and ran rampant with the Kelyn Pack as I called them. We didn't step on anyone's paws by circumventing the pack order; instead, we fell in behind the rest of the pack. Brightie sure did not like being last, but she was unusually gracious that day. I was sure I would pay the price down the line for her cordiality, but today was a special day, and I wasn't going to worry about that.

After we were all thoroughly exercised, Kelyn, Brightie and I were led to the driveway where Auntie Jan's SUV was parked. Uncle Don drove the car while my dad sat in the front passenger seat, my mom and Auntie Jan sat in the next row with Brightie in my mom's lap while Kelyn and I were in the back. Seemed like a proper arrangement since I heard we were going to South Carolina, and I didn't know how far that was from here.

Carly was tired from the events of the day before and wanted to stay home. Sidney didn't go due to his heightened anxiety level. He was okay with that arrangement and was content to stay with Beppe, who was older and set in his ways. Everyone in the SUV was excited, and anticipation filled the air as we left the driveway.

Was this another pilgrimage? I wasn't sure of anything at this point since I didn't know North Carolina from South Carolina, but I was a guest and really wasn't in any position to ask questions let alone complain. We reached a home of another one of the organization's puppy raisers, and she had planned a barbecue in my honor. Well, it might have been in honor of our whole family, but I liked thinking it was just for me. How many times does one meet up with a sibling lost in the world? This had to be another day dedicated to me. Could I be any more pompous? Probably not, but I was just going to go with the feelings of the moment.

We exited the SUV and were led into a huge yard. I thought my eyes were deceiving me. There were at least ten or twelve dogs running around the yard. They were either dogs in training for potential service or dogs who had been released from Puppy College. Nevertheless, there were a lot of them, and they were all having fun. This was a real backyard bonanza!

Kelyn, Brightie and I were released into the group of dogs. They were everywhere...traveling in a pack like a swarm of bees zigzagging through the yard. They stopped momentarily to acknowledge us and then encouraged us to join the group. We readily joined in the fun.

While Kelyn and I ran with the big dogs, Brightie met up with a pup named Milani who was around her own age. They decided to pair up and left the group to run and play on their own. They ran happily for quite some time and even found time to give the beautiful yellow day lilies lining the fence an unrequested haircut. Those pups ran rampant across the lines of flowers and relieved them of their floral tops. Their stomachs would suffer in the morning, but tonight was destined for fun and games. They were "Lilly-Pup-Shins" down to the last petal.

I ran with the big dogs for quite a while before exhausting myself. They crisscrossed around the yard too many times to count. I was fatigued and over stimulated. My system wasn't accustomed to so much running around. Dad recognized this and took me out of play. His taking me out saved face for me. It looked like he was ending it for me instead of my needing a break. What a guy!

He put my leash on me, walked me out of the play yard and onto the street. We walked a bit in the neighborhood and took some time to relax. We also sat on the curb momentarily while I regained my composure. Thanks to my dad, I was ready to rejoin the group on a much lower level of excitement.

Evening came upon us, and all of the dogs were very tired...including me. Brightie was sleeping soundly next to her playmate, and I was just about ready to doze off for a brief nap, when my attention was drawn to the gate.

A new dog happened to visit toward the end of the evening. As she glided through the gate, all heads turned. Her silken, blonde coat swayed as she walked. What a looker! I know I'm shameful when it comes to looking at female beauties, but I can't help myself. This dog was spectacular. Though she looked vaguely familiar, I couldn't quite place the face or where I had met her. Who was this radiant beauty?

She was definitely a Golden Retriever of the highest quality...had a rippling, blonde flowing coat that reminded me of sunshine on a cloudy day. Goofiness was overcoming me, but I couldn't help myself. She was just so dazzling. Her flaxen coat and snowy mask surrounding that perfect muzzle only accentuated her daunting, dark eyes that appeared to pierce right through me as she gazed in my direction. I angled my way over to her and discretely did some tentative sniffing. Continuing in this debonair manner, I told her that I was just a traveler here for the day and thought we had met somewhere before. My pickup lines weren't the best, but in my defense, I had very little practice. Just when I was going to give her another dim-witted line, I saw in her what was so familiar, and it scared me to death!

My mom was going to take a picture of this gorgeous blonde; but the minute the camera was aimed at her, this flaxen beauty moved her face to the side. She didn't like her picture taken...just like someone else I knew from my past.

*No pictures, please.*

It just couldn't be possible. I asked this beauty what her name was, and she demurely replied...Lulu. OMG! I was hitting on Linus' sister! I would pay dearly for this. Somehow he'd find out and come looking for me. I just knew it.

I withdrew a few paws away and inquired as to whether she had a brother named Linus who lived somewhere in the Midwest. She told me that she did, but they were separated when they were very young. He was sent to a family in that location, and she came to this family here in the South. She also heard that he was well and gaining quite a reputation for himself with his legendary method for canine socialization. She was very proud of him.

I told her that he and I had met, and that he was, without a doubt, a most innovative canine…way ahead of his time. We talked for a while about Linus, and she asked me to extend a heartfelt hello to him. I told her that I definitely would tell him all about her. Believe me, no more romantic thoughts crossed my mind about her. After all, she was someone's sister. That's really off limits…even to the most desperate of dogs! It's the canine law.

Lulu wanted to hear all about Linus, and I was anxious to tell her all about him and how he helped my family in so many ways. I also couldn't get over the striking resemblance between the siblings. It was uncanny. Except for the coloring of their coats, their features were identical. Add to that, they both didn't like their pictures taken. Go figure!

I also told Lulu that my mom would send a photo of her brother to her mom as soon as we got back home. She was so happy to hear that. While Lulu didn't usually like having her picture taken, she did allow my mom to take a special one to give to Linus. I assured Lulu that Linus would not only get her picture but hear all about her when we got back.

189

*Sending a smile across the miles.*

I was sorry we had to leave, but it was getting late. I reluctantly said goodbye to Lulu, and we all piled into the car for our return to North Carolina. We had much too much fun, and Brightie was so tired that she looked like a rag doll draped across my mom's lap. When we got to Kelyn's house, we transferred to our car and went back to the motel. We'd see each other tomorrow morning before we left for our journey home.

The next morning, after some playful running around in the yard with Kelyn's pack, it was time to say our goodbyes. It was such a wonderful trip, and seeing Kelyn meant so much to me. My mind was at peace knowing she was so loved. Even though we'd be apart, knowing she was safe was all that mattered.

I was to see Kelyn once again a few years later when my mom and dad rented a beach house on Topsail Island along the coast of North Carolina. We stopped to see Kelyn and her family while on our way home, and it was as though we had never been apart.

Sadly, Beppe, Sidney and Lulu had passed on to the Rainbow Bridge a few months earlier; and Martine, Tasha, Trixie and Briggs joined Kelyn and Carly in the pack. They had quite the family...lots of noise and an abundance of love. They are still a family held together by bonds of love and acceptance.

I never thought much about family or family bonds until that first visit with Kelyn and her pack. I learned a lot after spending just a few days with them. They were each very different, but they formed a family unit that prospered. Each dog added something special to the family, and each was better and stronger because of that allegiance to each other. It was a true lesson in family relationships.

I would do well to learn from that experience. We all left feeling especially good about our time spent with them, and I learned a most invaluable lesson. Working together, families can conquer just about anything. It wasn't until months later that I learned that actions speak louder than words...

## 16

# Unexpected Therapeutic Assistance

The months following our North Carolina trip were uneventful and yet passed so very quickly. Brightie went off to Puppy College, and I really missed my Get Me-Gimme Girl. The house was beyond quiet. I had no one to chase me around the yard or steal toys right out of my mouth. I allowed Brightie to get away with a lot of nonsense while she was with us, but that's what big brothers are supposed to do.

Before she left, I told her about my experiences at Puppy College and how challenging they were for me. While she was sorry to hear of my experiences, she wasn't worried about herself at all. She figured that they would either like her for the service gig, as she called it, or would not.

I sure wished that I had her attitude. Nothing phased that girl. We could pass a barking dog in close proximity while on a walk or a bird might land inches from her face, and she'd have no response. She just didn't expend energy on the minute distractions of the world.

A few months later, my mom received a call regarding Brightie. Although she had been approved physically as a breeder, her temperament left a lot to be desired. Apparently, Brightie's philosophy of service being another version of room service didn't set well with the organization. Their idea of service was very different from hers. Consequently, she was being released from the program for being assertive and somewhat defiant. Brightie? Assertive and defiant? That's my sister!

The folks gathered some things, put up the canvas crate in the back of the car, put me in my travel harness, and off we went to get Brightie. They were going to adopt her just as they had adopted me years ago.

It took about eight hours to get to Puppy College, and I have to admit that I freaked out when we pulled into the driveway. I had some bizarre thought that the folks were trading me in, and I'd have to stay there. Rather than shake off the wacky thoughts, I chose instead to flail around the back seat of the car. My frenzy resulted in my tangling myself in the travel harness and having to be rescued by my dad. While untangling me, he calmed and reassured me that we were just here at Puppy College to get Brightie.

Then I remembered how terrible I looked when my folks came to take me home. I was so frail and frightened that my mom cried much of the way home. Would today be a repeat of that terrible day? Would Brightie be frail? Would those daunting, dark chocolate eyes that drew the attention of every passing male canine be filled with sadness? Please, just let her be well.

It wasn't long before my questions were answered. As the front doors opened, my eyes were glued to the door. My mom came out first followed by Brightie. That dog strutted her way to the car as if she were leaving a canine day spa. If anything, she looked more stunning than ever.

*Brightie is so beautiful.*

She was definitely more mature looking and had filled out in all of the right places. There was something very striking about her that wasn't there before she matriculated to Puppy College. She had attained a level of self-confidence that most dogs only dream of reaching, and it showed in her demeanor. I envied that confidence, but I was also very grateful that she didn't seem to have any negative, residual effects from her Puppy College experience.

Brightie greeted me enthusiastically as she jumped into the car, and assumed a position next to me on the back seat. Going into the crate wasn't even a consideration for her. She was all grown up now, and the back seat was her throne, next to me, her newly adopted brother. *Newly adopted brother*? See how she turned things around? She was my newly adopted sister, but she didn't see it that way.

We talked a little about Puppy College and how marvelous the dogs were who were working toward service. She felt that she just didn't have that same level of dedication and knew she would never measure up to them. That was disappointing to her since she never backed down from any challenge; but service was important to the people who were helped, and she didn't want to short change them in any way. Brightie had scruples? Who was this dog, and what had they done with my Get Me-Gimme Girl?

Little did I know that she already had a plan in motion, and I was the key player. As the car left the driveway of Puppy College, I assumed my DOWN position on the back seat. Brightie sat next to the window and stared at the scenery as it flew by. She said very little which wasn't like Brightie at all. She and a chatterbox were usually one and the same. Was she mesmerized by the sights or just tired as a result of her stay at the kennels? I wasn't sure, but her silence made me very uneasy.

About an hour later, I heard whimpering and quickly sat up to see what was happening. There was Brightie seemingly frozen with fear as she sat looking out of the window. My first thought was that she was playing a trick on me and was trying to get me to look out of the window. It would be just like her to do that to me; I wasn't falling for it.

Of course, I made fun of her puppy-like attempt to lure me to the window, but she just sat frozen like a statue. She didn't move at all, and this was getting creepy. Maybe she did have some residual effects from Puppy College, and her confident attitude was just a show of false bravado on her part. Why did she have to be my adopted sister? Now, I had to do something.

I moved next to her as she continued to sit stone-like while staring out of the window. She didn't even seem to be blinking her eyes. Yikes! Double creeps! I talked softly to her and asked what I could do to help. After a while, she responded in a muffled tone that just sitting with her might help her overcome this unexpected bout with anxiety that seemed to come on so suddenly. She just didn't know what was happening to her, and all she could feel was fear.

By this time I knew she wasn't kidding me, but helping her meant facing my car window fear. She was my adopted sister; I had no choice. POWER TO THE PUP, POWER TO THE PUP echoed in my head as I ventured into the realm of my extreme phobia. Little by little, I forced myself to sit next to her while she sat facing the car window. My position next to her gave me a clear view of the countryside as it flew by, and nausea was slowly overtaking me. If dogs were able to turn green from nausea, I believe that color palette would be mine at this point.

Just when I thought I couldn't do this, Brightie leaned into me for support, and I felt her body relaxing as we sped down the highway. Forgetting the nausea, I leaned back for support and had a glimmer of hope that I was actually helping her. That was such a great feeling and so much stronger than the grip my window phobia held over me.

We sat next to each other, leaning closely for quite a few miles. Eventually, Brightie began talking to me. She asked me to describe the sights outside the car window since her fears seemed to obscure her view. I told her about the farm animals that dotted the meadows near the farm houses and how the landscape was changing as we sped closer to home. Restaurants, car dealerships, malls and gas stations replaced the farmlands. What astounded me was that as the miles passed, the views were no longer threatening to me. Instead, they were somewhat welcoming as we got nearer to home.

Brightie recognized my relaxed attitude by my tone of voice and graciously thanked me for helping in her time of need. She knew how serious my phobia was and how difficult it must have been for me to help her. I reminded her that we were family and that nothing else mattered. I would be there for her even if it meant facing my fears head on...just for her.

With that admission on my part, she turned her delicate head toward me, fluttered those curly eyelashes that surrounded those chocolate colored eyes and grinned. I immediately knew I had been fooled into facing my car window phobia. Brightie was up to her old tricks again. Whatever scruples she had while in Puppy College were left somewhere on the driveway as we hit the highway. Anger aside, I had to admit that once the nausea passed, seeing the countryside through the car windows was most enjoyable. It was so much better than staring at the car door from the DOWN position on the seat. While she did fool me, she did it for the right reasons. Nevertheless, it was a bit more evidence that I wasn't always the brightest bulb in the box.

I refused to talk to her for a while, but, eventually, got over it. Part of Brightie's charm was the fact that one couldn't remain angry with her for very long. Unfortunately, she knew it and used it to her advantage whenever possible.

When conversations resumed, she reminded me of her words of wisdom as we traveled to North Carolina months ago. I refused to look out of the car windows on that trip as well. At that time, Brightie told me that someday I would help someone in need and would face my fears for their sake. Back then, I thought that she was just talking nonsense, but that's exactly what I did for her today. According to her, she just moved up the helping timeline and gave me some unexpected therapeutic assistance.

All in all, this was quite the ride home from Puppy College. Brightie was back as my officially adopted sister, and I was finally looking out car windows. I'd have to reserve my mantra, POWER TO THE PUP, for something much more serious.

Everything in my life had really been so easy for me. The bond with Brightie had helped me to overcome a major phobia. My life was quite the life of leisure and a bit of a free ride. I was fed, brushed, exercised, sung to every night and unconditionally loved by a wonderful family. What more could a dog want?

However, wants and needs sometimes came with an eventual price. My mom mentioned something about no such thing as a free lunch. Brightie and I only ate twice a day so lunch wasn't even an option for us anymore. That fact made our mom's words somewhat confusing. What I later learned was that her words had absolutely nothing to do with lunch at all. Apparently, everything came with a price, and it was our time to pay...

## 17

# Service With A Smile

Returning home from Puppy College with Brightie was quite overwhelming in a number of ways. She was most helpful in terms of assisting me with my car window phobia, and for that, I'd always be grateful. However, since she wasn't in training for service anymore, the regular house rules now applied to her as well.

The first order of business was the pack order. As alphas of the pack, our folks did everything before we did. They ate their meals before we did, were first out of the door and always had the final word. I was next in the pack order, so it stood to reason that Brightie would follow me.

That didn't sit well with Brightie. Her first inclination was to use the "ladies first" approach which didn't even stand a chance with me. When she was young, I stopped myself from retaliating when she chewed on my face because she was a lady, but pack order was very different and not gender specific. I was here first, and she would just have to follow. What can I say…we agreed to disagree and decided to settle it the canine way.

For the next week or so, we jaw sparred, air snapped, tumbled around and chased each other in an attempt to get the other to roll over and show signs of submission. We were both very strong willed, and pack order is determined by strength, stamina and fitness. I wasn't about to give in to her fluttering eye lashes or demure looks from across the room. We were in this for the duration of our lives, and I wasn't going to give in to her feminine wiles. I must say, she was quite good; and if she weren't my adopted sister, she may have had an advantage over me. I wasn't going to fall for her girlie routine since I knew all of her tricks.

About two weeks later, as we were tumbling around in the back of Sparky 2 and vying for a position by the window of all places, Mom finally couldn't take it anymore. She stopped the car, turned to face us and instructed us to end the foolishness, or she would end it for us. Then we'd both be at the end of the pack.

We never heard such a harsh tone from our mom before, so we knew that she meant business. Since Brightie had no intention of sharing any position, she took the high road. She pranced into the middle of the back of the car and made a spectacle of rolling over in submission. All that was missing was applause. I was now the official leader of the canine pack. As I assumed a pose of regal stature, she made some reference to letting me win, but I didn't care.

Little did she know that if our mom hadn't stepped into the fracas, I would have given up. Battling day after day with Brightie was exhausting. At least now I could get some well-earned rest. I'm just glad there weren't any other dogs vying for positions in the pack. The outcome might not have been quite so positive for me. After all, I'm a thinker not a brawler!

Life settled into a pleasant routine of eating, sleeping, running around the yard and going for daily walks. It was most enjoyable. However, as we would soon learn, not all things enjoyable are long lasting. Our mom decided that we were wasting our talents and prior training as working dogs by not actually working at something. Here's where "there's no such thing as a free lunch" entered into the picture of our lives. We had to do something to earn our keep. It was decided that we would be re-trained as therapy dogs. While we couldn't be of assistance to one person, perhaps, we might help a group of people. Where did she get these ideas?

Since I was the eldest, I would go into the training program first. Brightie was supposedly still recovering from her stay at Puppy College. *Was missing her spa date making Brightie sad?* She was no more recuperating than I was having a mental breakdown. In human form, Brightie might have been a grifter and a good one at that. She was very good at fooling people; but she didn't fool me anymore, and she knew it.

Anyway, this therapy gig seemed appealing to me especially since I'd be working as a team with my dad. This was going to be fun. He'd let me do some things that my mom wouldn't allow. It was a guy thing, and my mom just wouldn't understand.

We went to the Therapy Dog Training Classes. I already knew the obedience portion, but I wasn't one for doing tricks, so I had to rely upon my friendliness and willingness to please. Now, that was a true stretch of the imagination. We forged onward and worked on proper greetings. I might have been a bit too enthusiastic. People in wheel chairs might not want a seventy pound therapy dog crawling into their laps. I had a lot of work to do in that area and in some other areas as well.

I learned how to eat pieces of hot dogs or green beans from a plastic fork since some children might be fearful of giving me a treat from their hand. A fork provided a safe method of treating, and I thought that to be quite ingenious. Bowling with Styrofoam pins and a rubber ball was a fun game, but sometimes I decided to run around the room with one of the pins in my mouth. Might I add, that was frowned upon. There was also work to be done on solving brain teaser puzzles, standing while being brushed and just being willing to offer comfort care...without landing on any laps. It was all service with a smile.

Despite all odds and a lot of practice, we passed the final test for registration as a therapy team. All we had to do was find a suitable program for our volunteer work. My dad and I made a great team. We tried a few programs, but the one that suited me best was the library reading program. Young children made a six week commitment to read to a dog every Saturday morning for fifteen minutes. They would bring their own books or select something the librarian had on the shelf, settle down on the blankets brought by the teams and read whatever material they chose...to the dog. It was a non-judgmental period of time where child and dog interacted entirely on their own with each other. The handler was only there to hold the leash.

I really enjoyed my library time; and each Saturday, six different children read to me. Some would read while petting me or having their arm around me; some might even scratch my stomach while they read. The children, who were a bit apprehensive about reading to me, might begin their reading time at the very farthest point of the blanket but would end up next to me by the end.    I learned so much about the *Diary of a Wimpy Kid, Judy Moody, White Fang* and many others. Some children even brought travel brochures.    They talked about their vacations and even described the pictures to me. Each week, I learned more and more about books and expanded my cranial capacity.    This volunteering was fun, and I even got to wear a cape.  I no longer thought of my cape as being magical; it now made me feel really important and proud to wear it.

*It was a matter of pride.*

I think Brightie was a bit envious of the days I went to the library, and pretty soon she was in the Therapy Dog Training Classes. She breezed through the program and even learned a few tricks in addition to regular games. The children seemed to like it when she played the toy piano. It just sounded like a lot of banging on the keys to me, but I don't have an ear for music, so I am not the best judge of her musical talents.

By this time, we were both in the library program and having a lot of fun while the children read to us.

*Team Players.*

209

Brightie wasn't much of a "morning dog" and often fell asleep during the reading time, but my mom would nudge her a bit just to wake her up at least when the child was reading to her.

There were times when Brightie was at her best. Those were the days when Rufus, the Parson's Jack Russell Terrier, was part of the library team for that scheduled day. She was definitely smitten with this suave and debonair canine companion. He wasn't just easy on the eyes either; Rufus was smart as a whip.

*Rufus was one talented terrier.*

He would do a high five and twirl around on command. If his team member pretended to sneeze, Rufus would grab a tissue from the tissue box and delicately give the tissue to his handler. He was quite the catch, and Brightie pulled out all of the stops to attract his attention.

He, too, seemed interested in her, and they would often share friendly greetings or linger after the reading sessions ended. I suppose some might say they were a "couple" in the strangest sense of the word. I just thought it was an odd relationship.

In addition to the library program's responsibilities, we'd often volunteer at festivals, holiday gift wrapping as well as the organization's information booths at numerous dog walks. We'd stand in front of the booth, and our mom and dad would talk about the organization, answer questions and even give demonstrations of what therapy dogs do for people. We'd work in shifts and often get an opportunity to see other dogs in the programs.

The volunteering for gift wrapping was always fun. Dogs worked in shifts with their handlers. While people had their holiday gifts wrapped, they could interact with the dogs. Brightie and Rufus often teamed up together for this event.

*Quite the gift wrapping team.*

They were real show stoppers as a "couple." Go Figure!

Brightie often looked for Rufus at the volunteer dog walks; and most times, he was there and eager to see her. I also knew that Rufus had a bit of a roving eye for the lady canines. I suspected that Brightie was not his only special friend. I would never say anything to Brightie about my suspicions since that was something she'd have to learn on her own.

On one of the Dog Walk Volunteer Days, Brightie, Rufus and I were just hanging around the information booth getting ready for the next shift to take over for us. Rufus and Brightie were whispering sweet nothings to each other while I prepared to leave. All of a sudden, a petite Cavalier King Charles Spaniel came into view of our booth. Apparently, she was the next shift at the booth, and Rufus could not take his eyes off this diminutive beauty. As hard as Brightie tried, she could not redirect his attention to her. She was being dumped because of this elfin, munchkin dog, and Brightie knew it. As we made our way to the car, I saw Brightie turn one more time to see if Rufus would perhaps give her a glance, but it didn't happen. Obviously, they were no longer a "couple."

The car ride home was very quiet, and any attempt to strike up a conversation with her was ignored. This had never ever happened to Brightie before; she was always the star attraction every place we went. While difficult for her to accept, it was just another one of life's lessons learned the hard way.

I tried to console Brightie by reminding her that while the Cavalier King Charles Spaniel was indeed a looker, she was quite small and according to big dog standards in the big dog world, anything smaller than a football was not actually a real dog. Consequently, she really didn't lose Rufus to another dog...just to a semblance of one. I don't think that made Brightie feel any better. What can I say? I'm just not skilled in sensitivity training and have probably alienated the entire small dog population just to make my adopted sister feel better about being dumped. Small dogs around the world, please forgive me. My words of consolation were for a good cause. They were meant to heal not to hurt.

Brightie's sadness didn't last very long. When we got home, the people next door had friends visiting from Colorado, and they brought their dogs…two distinguished Bernese Mountain Dogs. They immediately ran to greet Brightie. Once again, she was the star attraction and feeling good about herself. Life sure has a way of filling in the sadness blanks with happy things. It just proves that life takes care of us in spite of our mistakes or misadventures.

We continued with the volunteering for quite a while and always tried to be upbeat when we worked with the children. There was something special about the way they read to us. At the very least, they deserved service with a smile.

As therapy dogs, Brightie and I also did training demonstrations at the high school level as well as in the elementary grades. I had done assistance dog demonstrations when I was in training for service, but since we were re-trained a bit differently for assisted therapy, we demonstrated both training methods to the psychology students who were studying various types of learning styles. We also added a dog safety element to the presentations in the elementary grades. All in all, I think it went very well. The high school students thought we were so talented, and the elementary children thought we were so cool.

Brightie was very good at her parts, and I provided the comic relief. It was fun, and our mom and dad were able to talk about the importance of therapy dogs as well as the greater importance of volunteering for a good cause.

All of these events kept us pretty busy. Just when things were settling down at home, I heard my mom talking about advanced opportunities for us involving various, specialized activities. Now, what were we going to end up doing? Unfortunately, it wasn't long before we found out.

According to our mom and dad, all work and no play made for dull dogs, and so our rise from the mundane to some unspecified level of achievement began. Their intentions were good, and their expectations were high in terms of enjoyment for us. However, every now and then, outcomes don't quite measure up to the plans, and sometimes they even backfire...

# 18

## Agility Rocks

Please allow me to state my position on exercise in the life of a dog. Exercise is definitely a necessary component in a dog's daily life, but all things considered, moderation is the key. That's my position, and I'm sticking to it...at least for now.

The library reading program ended for the summer, and just when I thought this was the perfect time for some well-deserved rest and relaxation, the Exercise/Fun Speed Dial twirled and landed on GO. My mom had found the perfect fun activity that we could all do together. This activity would not only provide exercise, enjoyment and sharpen our obedience skills, but it would also strengthen the bond between dog and handler as well. Do we want fun? Absolutely. Do we need honing of our obedience skills? Most assuredly. But honestly, do we really need more exercising and bonding? If we got any more limber or closer, we'd all be joined at loosely aligned hips. As usual, either I missed the voting or was not included because we were all going to get involved in my mom's latest endeavor.

Her answer to the perfect team activity was Rally Obedience. For those who aren't familiar with Rally Obedience or Rally-O, it is a team sport for dogs and handlers. They work together following a course made up of obedience commands at various check points. The team stops at each designated position; the handler reads the commands on the sign since the dog can't read, gives the commands to the dog and the dog responds accordingly. Scoring involves the dog's accuracy of response to the commands, the handler's techniques and the team as a whole. A second level of stress is added...it's timed!

It sounded not only a bit too technical for me, but also demanded a huge amount of discipline and speed on my part. I liked to take my time with commands, and this situation called for an entirely different approach. Nevertheless, I decided to put my pessimistic attitude aside for the sake of the group and ventured into this new activity with the full intention of participating as best as I could.

Off we went to this new training facility that offered this class in Rally-O for Beginners. Our teams were established; I would work with my dad since I believed that he shared my same feelings about the class. We made a good team. Brightie, being her enthusiastic self, couldn't wait to get started and would work with our mom, who was the cheerleader for this activity; we were going to have fun together…even if it were the last thing we did.

The training facility was pretty nice and quite large. Rubber runners formed a course for us to follow. There were a few numbered signs on which commands were written, and they were placed at various locations around the course. All in all, it didn't look too difficult. After all, it was the first class.

Of the six dogs in the class, Brightie, a Miniature Schnauzer and I were the beginners. The Doberman Pincher, the Collie and the Golden Retriever were taking the class to sharpen their skills for future competitions. They each had already received awards in this type of class. I considered them to be "ringers," and my stress level immediately jumped a notch. After all, this was supposed to be a beginner's class. We, the beginning three, would look like fools while they already knew what to expect. I just didn't like the odds starting out of the gate.

Anyway, the class began, and we were instructed in the rules, the course and proper ways of following the directions on the signs that dotted the floor of the course. Since it was the first class, each sign contained only one command. Later, the signs would have two or three commands, but I didn't have to worry about that yet.

As we lined up, the instructor had the "ringers" go first. I figured as much. They could probably do the course blindfolded at this point. However, watching each of the three dogs go through the course was really somewhat inspiring. These were really skilled pooches, and I understood the reasoning in sending them first. We saw how it was done and how to do it correctly. That made sense to me and was met with my approval.

My mom and Brightie went next, and Brightie was at her best. Her SITs were crisp, DOWNs were swift and her right and left turns looked like she was using a protractor to get the angles correct. She was at the top of her game and having a blast. My mom was very pleased with their first attempt at the course.

My turn was next and I have to admit that my SITs weren't the best and my DOWNs were a bit slow. I did get right from left correct, but not as angular as required. My dad really tried to cover for me; but all in all, our performance lacked polish. However, he praised me and carried on about what a great routine we did together as a team. He sure knew how to make a dog feel good, but I think his nose grew a bit longer after that pup talk.

The weeks progressed, and the course became considerably more difficult. Two and three commands were at each station, and the clock was ticking. My mom and Brightie still shined in the competition, and my dad and I just wanted to get through the course with the least amount of embarrassment. So far, we were accomplishing our goal.

The last class was actually a mock competition. We would follow a regulation course, be timed and scored as though it were an actual competition. Tension was high. By this time, the "ringers' just seemed pompous; but while I knew that I personally didn't have much of a chance of winning, I had my bets on Brightie. She was top notch and had given them a run for their dog treats during the last few classes. She had accuracy and speed...something I didn't demonstrate unless I was being chased.

The competition began, and the "ringers" went first. Their scores were good, and their times were pretty fast; but I believed that Brightie was faster. My dad and I completed the pretty difficult course in a suitable time but nothing competitive. I was just glad that we finished with reasonable scores. I wasn't the screw up I imagined I'd be in the competition.

It was then Brightie's turn, and she and my mom whizzed through the course with reckless abandon. One of the turns was slightly off due to their speed, but both of them were amazing to watch. They were a beginning team and were matching the "ringers" in both accuracy and speed. As it turned out, my mom and Brightie came in second by two points. I demanded a recount, but no one listened. It was still an honor for my mom and for Brightie. You Go Girls! I was just grateful that the sessions were over and we could resume our lazy living at home once again. How could one dog be so wrong...so many times?

While we participated in the Rally-O experiences with feigned enthusiasm, little did we know that there were more to come. Our mom figured that while Rally-O was good for us, it didn't offer the excitement she was hoping to find for us. If I had the ability to communicate in words, I would have told her that she had gone above and beyond for us. We were very happy the way we were. There was no need for her to find other avenues for our enjoyment. Needless to say, that type of communication was not possible, and her quest for our enjoyment persisted.

This time, her venture took the form of Agility for Beginners. We went to the same facility as the Rally-O classes. Now, the command signs were replaced by hurdles, open and closed tunnels, see-saws, weave polls, elevated hoops and platforms. This was an amusement park in itself, and the possibilities were endless. Mom had hit the jackpot with this class. Agility rocked!

*Fun time!*

Once again, there were six of us in the class, but this time we were all beginners. The course was relatively easy at first, but it would get progressively more difficult and would include more obstacles. For now, we used a few hurdles, an open and closed tunnel and a platform. It seemed simple enough, and we were kept on our leashes.

I was once again paired with my dad. Since my folks used hurdles and a regulation tunnel at home when I was a puppy, I had prior experience with some of the equipment. As a result, it didn't seem like much of a challenge. However, the closed tunnel wasn't my favorite. I liked to see where I was going, and not seeing an opening at the end of this tunnel gave me concern...enough so that I wouldn't go through it. After a few attempts, I eventually shut my eyes and bolted through the closed opening.

As usual, Brightie was excellent at all of this and followed my mom's directions with or without a leash. I continued to be leashed, probably for my own protection, since I often lost concentration while running around the course. Sometimes, I just found a shortcut to avoid the closed tunnel and swerved off towards hurdles or the see-saw...much to my dad's dismay. Inventing new patterns was fun, and wasn't having fun the objective in taking this class? Apparently, deviating from the course was not up for discussion, nor was it appreciated. Being a free spirit wasn't exactly encouraged in this venue.

While the closed tunnel might have been something for me to avoid, the see-saw held my interest on a number of levels. It had the up and down capability that was both startling on the way up yet exhilarating on the way down. It was double the fear or double the fun. It all depended upon one's perspective. There were folded towels under the boards at each end which were meant to absorb the impact of the see-saw as it took its downward bounce from the dog's weight. I just viewed them as props for future use. I was always thinking ahead, and this agility class fired my imagination once again. I wasn't just a dog following directions and running around through an obstacle course. I became an adventurer, meeting every challenge with the skill and finesse of a brave warrior.

As the classes continued, the course became more difficult, and the last class was a regulation competition. In this competition, we were to be unleashed. If that fact alone didn't instill apprehension in my dad, nothing would. If it did, he didn't let on. He just stood confidently with me while we waited for our turn to compete. I don't think he wanted his anxiety to travel down the leash.

My imagination spun into overdrive as I waited for our turn. Would I be a Knight of the Round Table fighting for my lady's honor, a skilled athlete hoping for Olympian glory or perhaps a NASCAR driver striving for record breaking times on the raceway? I would make my decision once I settled on the course, and my excitement grew as I waited to begin.

Brightie went first. She was unleashed and made no move until directed by my mom. When the signal was given, off they went at the speed of light. Brightie followed my mom's directions to the letter. There were no short cuts for that girl.

*Brightie was at her best.*

She went through the tunnels, over the hurdles, up and down the see-saw, through the weave poles and ended in perfect form on the platform. The last time I saw Brightie move that fast was when she saw a hot dog fall from a plate at our last barbecue. That girl could run! She scored a lot of points, and I could see the pride in my mom's face as she left the course with Brightie by her side.

Now, it was my turn. As my dad and I approached the starting point, I had already decided what persona would rule this course. I was going to be Kessen, the record breaking NASCAR driver. As such, I was determined to break my own world record. Tension rose, and my hackles bristled with excitement as my dad removed my leash. The signal was given, and off we went. I followed my dad's directions through the tunnels, over the hurdles, through the weave poles and back around to the dreaded closed tunnel. I was fearless; I was Kessen the legendary race car driver. Without giving it a second thought, I blasted through the closed tunnel reaching the opening in record speed. I had just one more obstacle to complete on the course before I raced to the platform. That last obstacle was the see-saw. I could almost taste success. As I approached it, I made sure my paws landed on the correct spot to avoid any loss of points, went up and then down the other side. I declared myself a winner. If I had arms, I would have waved to the imaginary cheering crowds.

In hindsight, that winning declaration was my first serious mistake. Instead of continuing to the platform which signaled the end of the exercise, I chose to deviate from the plan. I turned toward the see-saw, much to my dad's dismay, and headed for the towel at the base. In my vivid imagination, I was a NASCAR driver and, against all odds, a winner. What does a winner do? He takes that well-earned victory lap or two...which was my second critical mistake of the event. I grabbed the towel from under the see-saw and began my victory laps around the course completely ignoring my dad's calling of my name. This was my third and final mistake.

I was lost in my own imagination. As that towel flew higher, my dad's spirits plummeted. I wasn't hearing him calling my name; I only heard the cheers and applause of the crowds as I took my laps with my victory flag signaling my success.

Of course, this was all going on in my head. While I knew I'd have to return to reality soon, I also recognized that I was in big trouble. One's imagination, while quite the wonderful thing, can be somewhat troublesome at times. This was definitely one of those times. I had hit the Jackpot...the Trifecta of Mistakes! Now, it was time to pay the price for those mistakes.

I was quickly brought back to reality by catching the glare from my mom's eyes as she stood at the far end of the course…with her hands on her hips. It was not a good sign at all. Realistically speaking, I hadn't expected one at this stage of the bedlam.

It wasn't that she was angry; it was something far worse. She was disappointed…not in me, but in what I had done in front of all of those people. Skidding to a stop in front of her and trying to look pathetic with a towel hanging from my mouth wasn't working. I attempted to look contrite by sitting perfectly still with my head down, but that towel in my mouth only made me look comical. As she held out her hand, I quickly dropped it into her extended palm. My victory flag existed no more. Without a word, my mom attached my leash and handed me over to my dad who was totally embarrassed by my actions. She took hold of Brightie's leash, and we left the facility without a word. We never returned.

The folks were all pretty embarrassed by my trip to adventure land on that agility course. As a side note, Brightie was laughing about what I had done, but she was still somewhat concerned about how much trouble I'd be facing when we got home. The ride home was silent. Not even the radio was on during the trip home. This was not a good sign.

I wished they would just yell at me and get it over with now rather than later. That wasn't their plan, and they never yelled at me anyway. They were going to drag this out until I couldn't stand it anymore, and I would beg for punishment. I just knew they were waiting for me to offer them some consequence far worse than what they would do to me. I was in trouble, and that was a fact. They had always been fair with me and with Brightie, but she rarely did anything wrong. The girl either lacked imagination, or she was smart enough to avoid being caught.

We got home, and still there was silence. It was creeping me out. Just get it over with...banish me to my kennel, or don't give me dinner. Wait, don't do that. Instead, yell at me. I could take it. However, no punishment was given other than the disappointed expression on my mom's face. I had never seen such a look of sadness before, and I was the cause of it. That hurt worse than any punishment they could have given me...even the no dinner thing. I slowly crept to my corner and hugged my toy for consolation.

My mom had done nothing but give me unconditional love for all of my life, and how had I repaid her? I embarrassed her in front of everyone in the class. I'd been foolish in the past, but not with anything of importance. The Agility Class was important to my mom in the sense that she thought of it as not only enjoyment for us but a way to extend the bond that already existed between all of us in the family. I had truly disappointed her and would probably never find a way to make it up to her.

*I'm not proud of my behavior.*

I'll never forget the look of disappointment and sadness and on her face that day and how sad it made me feel. I had done that to her, and she had done nothing but make me feel good about myself for my entire life. I'd like to say that I would never do such a thing again, but in all honesty, I couldn't promise that. What I did promise is that I would try to be the dog she believed I could be. That's a promise I definitely could, and would, keep for the rest of my life.

Time heals all wounds; and, by the next day, all was well. The folks never did hold a grudge before, and they didn't start now. I even thought I heard them laughing about it the night before, but I couldn't be sure of that. Brightie and I no longer took additional classes for bonding or for enjoyment. Instead, we relied upon daily walks and running around the yard as our daily exercise. As I said before, exercise is a vital part of a dog's daily routine, but moderation is definitely the key.

Things went back to normal, and we assumed a routine that suited everyone. We ate, slept, played, walked outside, ran around the yard, ate and slept some more. It was perfect for us. At the end of each day, we looked forward to our mom's ritual of singing to us. She had done this for years and would continue to do it for years to come. Brightie and I were lucky dogs!

A few weeks later, Brightie and I noticed some changes in the house's layout. Gates were now situated in various parts of the house, and the small kennel that we had both used when we first arrived here was now positioned in the same place as it was then. While these were all significant signs of change, the real warning light went off in both our heads with the positioning of the small, elevated stand containing a set of water and food bowls. This was the most ominous sign in terms of change since we both knew what it meant. A roller coaster ride of significant proportion awaited us. It would, in fact, change our lives forever...

# 19

## Marnie Google

It was winter now, and snow had already fallen. It created such a wonderland of fun for us. Brightie usually didn't like to get her paws wet, but jumping around in the snow was a different story. She loved the snow; and the deeper it was, the better it was for her.

*The Snow Queen.*

Fortunately for me, it was the only time I could out run her. Escaping her clutches was easily accomplished in the snowy end of the yard.

We had a record breaking snowfall so far this year, and the dog run was continuously covered with deep, heavy snow. Dad's task was to shovel an area of the dog run for us...even if it meant getting up in the middle of the night to do it. He was meticulous about that. His philosophy was that if it got too deep, it would only be more difficult to shovel in the morning. In the middle of the night, he could be heard out there shoveling. While we were certainly grateful, we often just dove into the deepest part for the fun of it.

We heard that our Auntie Deb and Auntie Brenda were coming to stay with us which meant that our folks were going out of town for a few days. We didn't know where they were going. We just knew that we were in for some excitement with our puppy sitters. We couldn't wait for the "sniffing game" to begin as well as all of the hugs and kisses we got from them. Great fun awaited us while the folks were traveling to who knows where.

We had already forgotten about the changes in the house in terms of the positioning of the small kennel and installation of the gates. Nothing happened, and no change in our daily routines occurred. We thought it was just a false alarm in our heads. In hindsight, how could two dogs be so wrong...so often?

The folks had only been gone overnight, and we were surprised the next day when we heard their car pull into the driveway. We both went to our assigned positions for greetings and waited for the door to open.

*Our hackles tingled with anticipation.*

As it slowly opened, a scene reminiscent of the past flooded my brain. It was happening all over again, and I didn't know if I could handle it. Fear overcame me. As a result, I slowly backed away from the door and ran into my safe place...the corner. I hoped beyond hope that I was seeing things and that my imagination was playing tricks on me. That had to be it. With that possibility in mind, I left my safe place and cautiously returned to the greeting area near the door.

Brightie didn't know why my reaction was so strange since all she saw was my mom holding a beautiful puppy in her arms. This was something to be celebrated and not feared. She didn't realize how traumatic her very own arrival had been a few years ago. Brightie only remembered the sunshine; I remembered the pain. I stood warily off to the side, allowing for a quick escape in case it was needed.

The folks entered and introduced the little pup as Marnie. She was an eight week old, full Labrador Retriever and was also in training for potential assistance just as we had been. I suppose she would be considered another so-called sister to me. It was becoming a sorority house around here with all these females. The puppy's appearance was striking due to her soft, coal-black, shiny coat. Her expressive eyes were as dark as her coat, yet they seemed a bit too large for her tiny face. She had an impish look about her in spite of her wrinkled face, and I had to admit that it was quite disarming. In her own way, she was breathtaking, and so far, not in a scary way. However, it was still too early in the game to tell.

As I recalled the first night with Brightie, that honeymoon only lasted a few hours before the aria of howling and screeching began. I was cautiously optimistic about this situation. I would give this little pup a chance, but I had learned through past experience to keep my face out of biting distance.

Mom put Marnie down on the floor, and she timidly came to greet Brightie. The pup was a bit fearful and not at all like someone I know whose greeting included taking a huge chunk out of my face. I won't mention names, but the perpetrator was in the room sitting next to me. Brightie eagerly sniffed the puppy as a sign of welcome, and the greeting was happily returned. I tentatively approached the new arrival and was pleasantly surprised when she rubbed up against me choosing to nuzzle my face instead of bite it. Perhaps this puppy would work out after all and not have all of the drama of the resident Diva, a.k.a. Brightie. At least this pup came with built in manners.

Now Brightie did not know what I was talking about in terms of horrible meetings. She remembered her first meeting as one of love and understanding. That girl needed a reality check. She only remembered what was convenient. No one wants to remember being thought of as possessed, needing an exorcist or having to be checked every day for the numbers 666 on one's body. Remembering the good stuff and blocking out the rest made for better sleeping habits.

I had to admit that this puppy sure was a cutie.

*Marnie seemed delightful.*

She had some pretty big paws for such a petite pup, but one didn't notice them at first. Her eyes were her money makers. Those eyes and that angelic expression could melt frozen dog treats. I knew I had to give her a chance, but I'd let Brightie take the lead on this. Since Linus had passed on to the Rainbow Bridge a few years ago, we had no life line of defense. We were on our own with this little tyke, and I still couldn't make my lips quiver without laughing. Linus was a true master of the lip quiver.

Dad had already cleared an area in the dog run for Marnie, and we all made our way outside into the cold weather which didn't seem to bother her at all. The snow had been so deep that it would have covered her completely if it hadn't been shoveled. Way to go Dad!

But what did that little rascal do? She took a running start on the deck, thrust her front paws forward and dove into the deep end of the snow. She looked like a black bundle sticking out of the white snow.

Marnie waded around in the snow, did what she had to do and came running back into the house. Mom dried her off and sent her happily into the kennel that had once been ours. Nice to know that our puppy kennel passed from generation to generation. We were part of history, and we didn't even know it until now.

Marnie settled down quickly on a nice warm blanket surrounded by some toys and had the luxury of some soothing music. Our mom had ordered some puppy lullabies and began playing them after Marnie entered her kennel. Brightie and I assumed sentry duty on either side of the kennel in case Marnie woke up and was frightened. The distinct possibility also existed that she would wake up howling and not let up until morning. Someone else I know did that, but I won't mention her name. Anyway, the lullabies not only put Marnie to sleep, but we quickly followed suit. That music was powerful stuff.

Interestingly enough, Marnie did not get up howling. Mom woke her up in the middle of the night to go outside, which I thought was asking for trouble, but my mom knew what she was doing. After all, she raised us. Marnie once again jumped into the deep snow avoiding the cleared section that our dad worked so hard to prepare for her. As quickly as she ran out, she was back and sound asleep. Thank goodness, this one seemed to be a sleeper. The music was a big help as well.

Marnie's training began immediately since she had to learn her name along with other commands. Responding to her name was first on the list. She was a fast learner.

Whenever our mom said her name and Marnie looked at her, she got a treat. Although we were just spectators on the other side of the gate, we did get a treat once in a while. We knew it was part of our meals, but it was still a treat. While Marnie didn't know that she was being shortchanged a part of her meals for learning commands, we weren't going to tell her. If we were found out to be snitchers, we might lose our treats as well. Brightie and I aren't brilliant; but with our combined intelligence, we had a good thing going.

I have to say that from the get-go, Marnie was an easy puppy to work with in the house. She didn't bite our faces and seemed to enjoy sparring with Brightie on a daily basis. I remained a spectator or, better yet, the supervisor of the canine socialization process. I still had nightmares about Brightie biting my face, so I was content with being on the sidelines of Marnie's training. Our mom handled the verbal commands while Brightie and I worked with the canine aspect.

When we saw that she was learning at an accelerated rate, we figured it was time to give her a nickname as a type of reward for a job well done. Each of us had earned a nickname when we were young. Now, it was Marnie's turn.

I had been given the name of K-Man, probably referring to my potential for special powers. After all, it was a nickname and not intended for an actual representation of my prowess. Brightie had been aptly dubbed Brightie Girl because even though she was rough and tumbling, she still had her girly, Diva ways. On the other hand, Marnie was a bit puzzling in terms of nicknaming her. She was good at everything. Something even closely accurate in describing her wouldn't seem like a nickname at all. We decided to go the wacky route and christened her Marnie Google since she had the goo-goo-goo- gliest eyes.

*The perfect nickname.*

We envied those spectacular eyes, and the best way to honor that was to kid her about them. While she loved her nickname, we loved her because of it.

Marnie was a gem in terms of learning with verbal commands as well as canine socialization. Although she did have one aspect of her learning that was less than acceptable and definitely less than feminine; she was a top notch food gobbler.

Every morning at meal time, Marnie would greet us enthusiastically around the food bowls. She definitely had manners and never ventured into our food space, but that's where any appearance of etiquette vanished. She was a food gobbler and took food gobbling to an art form. Since she was a growing girl, she had a lot more food in her bowl than we did. If inhaling food were a gift, she had it. Brightie and I marveled at her inhalation technique. This girl could eat!

Gobbling is not the best method for food intake. Our mom tried a number of different techniques to quell the zest for food in that little lady. Mom tried a type of bowl that had a pedestal in the center that was supposed to slow down the eating process. Marnie only gulped food faster and learned to work her head in a circular motion. Then, there was the silver ball put in the bowl that Marnie was to roll around in order to get at her food a bit slower. Our little girl could maneuver, and that ball didn't have a chance. Next, there was hand feeding. A few morsels of food would be in hand; and when the morsels were consumed, others took their place. Well, that might have worked for a short period of time, but hand feeding was not time efficient and wouldn't work for Marnie when she went to Puppy College. While the food intake method might have been solved with a food dispensing ball, potential service dogs were not allowed to eat anything from the floor. That ball was the most practical option, but it wasn't even a consideration due to Marnie's future goals.

One has to understand that all of Marnie's training was preparation for her future service endeavor. Something had to give in terms of quelling her gulping. Mom then tried putting a few morsels of her food in the bowl so Marnie could eat and digest what was in front of her. That worked, but it was still a process that wouldn't work in the kennels later in her training. After attempting all of those possible solutions, our mom went with the most daring one. She decided to do nothing...absolutely nothing. If Marnie chose to gulp her food and sometimes, forgive me for saying this, throw up and have a second serving of the same food, well so be it. There were bigger hills to climb and greater battles to fight in the future. Food gulping was not a high priority. Way to Go, Mom!

In the weeks and months that followed, Marnie got along well with us but especially with Brightie. They were closer in age and had a lot more energy than I had. Every day after our first wild run around the yard, I ventured off into a shaded area under a tree to eat grass and possibly throw up while they faced imaginary foes hiding behind shrubs…much like I did when I was young. I envied their energy, but I also knew there were no foes hidden in the shrubbery. They were chasing day dreams, and that was okay for them. I was just grateful that I wasn't expected to join in their escapades.

*Marnie's yard escapades were exhausting.*

Marnie was special in so many ways. What was consistent about her was that she was devoted to whoever was within her sights. While she loved both people and dogs, I do believe she loved people more. She adored my mom and followed her wherever Mom went in the house...without a tether. When we needed a reality check due to ridiculous behavior, we were occasionally tethered to our mom by a bungee-like leash. Marnie stayed by our mom's side without any type of leash. That was incredible as far as I was concerned. Giving up playing with us to sit next to our mom while she read a book was bizarre. The girl needed serious help.

Marnie wasn't licking up to the adults. She had her canine play time and played hard when out in the yard with Brightie. She also reigned in her excitement levels to adjust to human behavior and expectations. Her public behavior was most acceptable...especially in church. We all know I had some dubious moments in church, but she outshined us all. Marnie was an example for dogs in training everywhere.

To be honest, Brightie and I were very proud of Marnie. She was everything we wanted to be but couldn't. She loved doing things for others and never wanted anything in return...which was a concept we never quite understood. We worked for food; she worked for the fun of working.

*The girl loved housework.*

One of the most endearing qualities that Marnie possessed was making each of us feel special. With Brightie, she always let her go first in whatever they were doing. They never squabbled about who got there first or who needed it more. Marnie always conceded to Brightie. In return, Brightie taught Marnie the intricacies of play engagement. She was taught to play bow, spin around twice and bark. Our mom was not always pleased with Brightie's approach to mentoring.

With me, it was something very different. I didn't have any control issues, and Marnie could have run all over me on a daily basis, but she didn't. From the first minute of her arrival, she used me as a sort of building block for seeing the world. Visibility was an issue for her due to her small stature, so she used me for her view into the day's adventures.

Each day when our mom was getting meals ready, Marnie would stand on her hind legs and put her front paws on my back. She would not only balance herself, but also see what was going on higher up towards the counter top. The girl knew strategy, problem solving and, apparently, the easiest way to see objects out of one's sight. Whenever she needed a better view of anything, she'd prop herself up on my back. I, of course, would let her. She was a bit of a canine phenomenon, and our own treasure of a friend.

The year passed quickly, and Marnie sailed through her public outing phase with ease. It was winter again. As her time to matriculate to Puppy College grew closer, Brightie and I dreaded that occurrence. Marnie had become not only a friend but part of our family, and we were going to miss her. I knew Marnie had everything that Brightie and I didn't have...the will to work and to please others.

When our folks took her off to Puppy College, I had the feeling that I would never see her again. It wasn't because she disappeared into some training void but because I knew that she would rise above all expectations and turn out to be the assistance dog we believed she could become. We missed her terribly when she left.

*Will Marnie ever come back?*

Brightie showed it more than I since they were closer in age and played so much more on a daily basis. Brightie lay at the back door, off and on, for almost a week after Marnie matriculated. Brightie only left that spot briefly to look out of the front window in case she missed Marnie's return through the back door. I, on the other paw, kept watch for her at the front door.

I missed her very much but kept my feelings to myself. In my heart, I somehow knew that I would never see her again. She was destined for service, would learn the most from Puppy College and go on to assist someone who needed the help of a fun loving dog. Marnie was such a special dog. She was devoted to helping others, had the most incredible eyes, and apparently, loved people more than dogs. That was our Marnie.

Marnie never did come back to us. She graduated from Puppy College and went on to a new owner who gained not only her assistance but her love as well. It was as it should be in terms of the puppy raising process, and we had to accept that.

We missed our good friend, our Marnie Google, but knew she was doing what she was meant to do. While we weren't able to achieve her type of success, we were so very happy and proud to have been a part of her journey.

*Our special friend.*

What could be more appealing than this? Marnie was our very own success story. The gates were down, and the multi-generational kennel was put into storage once again. All that was ahead of us was rest and relaxation, or so we thought. Our folks, however, had other things in store for us.

Brightie was going off to spend time with Auntie Deb and Auntie Brenda, and I was going on a road trip via Route

66 to California with the folks. How much fun could that be? One would think that it might be considered a trip back to my roots. After all, I had been born in California and hadn't returned since I was eight weeks old. Going back to my roots across the country made me somewhat of a cross country canine. That was a bit exciting even for me. It was going to be the road trip of all road trips. Thanks to Brightie's therapeutic intervention months ago, I was even going to look out of the windows during the entire trip. Occasionally road trips don't turn out to be as wonderful or as exciting as planned. Sometimes what starts out as a dream come true becomes a nightmare of the utmost proportion....

## 20

# Cross Country Canine

The only scene more beautiful than sunrise in the shadows of the Santa Rosa Mountains of California is the radiance of the sunset. I know dogs aren't supposed to notice such things, but this canine appreciated the inherent beauty of the landscape. The scenery rekindled the memories of my very first home. Now, here in California, I was back to relive and reminisce. It was much needed closure.

The road trip to California was a bit uneventful. While the changes in the terrain were most noticeable as we progressed from state to state, there wasn't much adventure in the traveling. Rest stops varied in appearance, but the basics were always the same. Dog areas were nondescript, but served a purpose. That's all that counted as far as I was concerned.

At times, traveling on Route 66 was boring since there was really nothing for me to do except sleep.

Since my dad enjoyed driving, my mom learned to play the harmonica to occupy her time. Not even sleep spared me from that auditory experience.

*Are we there yet?*

From what I gathered, the harmonica wasn't the easiest to play, but my mom never gave up until she could play a number of songs...*The Battle Hymn of the Republic* and *Taps* were most notable or might I say, most recognizable in terms of melody. Everything else was a bit of a free for all, and I mean that in the kindest sense. The dissonant sounds did take away a bit of the monotony of the highway; and because of that, the harmonica symphony was a huge success.

*Starved for entertainment.*

Staying in different motels was fun. Some offered free breakfasts, and others didn't. That didn't concern me one way or another since I was on a people-food free diet. I had my dog food, and it, in no way, compared to the aroma of bacon and eggs, since my food has no aroma at all.

To be honest, I was feeling a bit shortchanged in the food department. At home, fresh vegetables were always mixed into my meals, but being on the road didn't allow for that; dry dog food only goes so far when it comes to enjoyment. Traveling had its sacrifices, and my less than savory food consumption was apparently one of them.

What I noticed most, in the cross country traveling, were the changes in the terrain. We left our area surrounded by deep, green foliage which eventually turned to dusty brown vegetation as we crossed from state to state. Mountains gave way to fiery, red, rock formations amidst the desert like conditions. Bushes were replaced by various forms of cactus plants; rest stops were fewer and farther apart.

A bit of comic relief occurred when one of the anticipated rest stops was closed and the next one wasn't available for one hundred miles. Now, it didn't matter to me since I have a bladder like a camel, but it was not at all amusing to my mom who was counting on that rest stop being open. Dad really picked up the pace on the highway, and not a word was spoken until we reached the next rest stop…in record time.

All in all, the few days spent on the highway were without incident. In terms of safety, that was a good thing. We did see the World's Largest Thermometer in passing, but my mom didn't get her camera out in time to capture it into the digital history of the trip. We'd have to rely on our memories for that image. Brightie would have loved seeing that.

Finally reaching our California destination was exciting. We stayed at a posh, well known, time share resort that had all of the amenities of a five star hotel. In fact, one such hotel was adjacent to the property, and we were allowed to venture on to the premises at will. There were restaurants, pools, shops, galleries and musical entertainment to be enjoyed all day long. It was like living the life of the rich and famous; adventures were at our fingertips and paws.

We stayed in a time share villa on a golf course, and it had every possible convenience. It was like being at home but much classier. Everywhere we went, the sun shone brightly, and my daily walks were confined to very early morning jaunts because of the extreme heat. I appreciated the early morning start to my day probably more than my dad who took on the task. My mom needed rest from the rigors of car travel, and he was happy to accommodate. What a guy! Besides, walking early in the morning helped me sleep much better during the day...not that I needed much help in that area.

*Sleeping is my specialty.*

Venturing off the premises of the resort, we strolled the sidewalks of the famous El Paseo Drive, also known as the Rodeo Drive of the Desert. Its numerous, posh boutiques offered many opportunities for window shopping. My mom didn't purchase anything; but, according to her, window shopping was the fun of it all. I don't get it, but I don't have a choice since I am the one on the leash.

We also strolled the avenues of Highway 111. Often referred to as The 111, it had many restaurants and outdoor cafes. Each offered menus that awakened the drooling response in me. As compensation, I was offered water. While I was thankful, I still felt a bit shortchanged.

Back at the resort, we relaxed on the patio of our villa or by one of the many pools. I was the only canine at the pool, so I was a bit of a show stopper but became more of a novelty as compared to some of the bathing beauties in the area. I was handsome in a canine sort of way but couldn't compete for attention since the bathing suit competition was just too great.

Almost every day, we took trips to various areas outside of the resort. We went to a place called a Date Farm. When I first heard we were going to a Date Farm, I got pretty excited about the prospects. As it turned out it wasn't what I thought it would be. It was a farm for growing dates, and they were sold in the farm's store. Dates for all occasions such as baking or eating purposes were for sale. The farm even had a restaurant and sold frozen date yogurt. While it didn't sound appealing to me, I did get a taste, and it was quite refreshing. Of course, I didn't even know what a date was, so the flavor was foreign to me anyway. It was still tasty and a step up from water. After my mom bought some dates for a friend, we traveled back to the resort for some much needed rest and relaxation. Visiting a Date Farm in the heat of the day is in itself an exhausting endeavor but a most enjoyable one.

On another day, we went to a street fair where every possible type of jewelry, craft item or food delicacy might be purchased. Everything was so colorful, the people were so nice and the aromas again awakened the drooling demons in my mouth. I was surrounded by corn dogs, cotton candy and fried cakes. I was only compensated with water, but it was refreshing, and hydration is such an important aspect of one's health...or so I was told as I drooled in front of the popcorn machine. Aside from that, it was quite a remarkable day considering all of the sights, sounds and aromas.

In our travels to an Outlet Shopping Mall, we passed something called a Windmill Farm. I had never ever seen a farm like this. Miles and miles of unusual, pinwheel-like structures dotted the terrain as far as the eye could see. These strange looking structures were called windmills, and they were actually generating electricity from the wind. Who would have even imagined that possible? I learned so much from this trip and I'm just a dog. Imagine what people could learn! Since a farm for windmills was an entirely new concept for me, I did have some questions. How are these windmills grown? Are they grown from seeds; and if so, where do they get them? There were too many unanswered questions from this excursion.

*There's so much to think about on this trip.*

The week passed quickly, and we had a lot of adventures outside of the resort area. One most memorable was going to the church celebration on Sunday. The church was magnificent with its stained glass windows, and the structure was actually shaped like a cross. The pastor spoke eloquently and had a great sense of humor which I could tell from the laughter at some of his jokes. I didn't understand the punch lines, but the people did, and I guess that was all that counted. After all, I was just a guest who happened to be a dog. All in all, it was a nice ending to our week's stay. The next day, we would leave California and begin our journey home.

On our last night, as we sat on the patio and watched the sun setting in the shadows of the Santa Rosa Mountains, I couldn't help but remember my early days in California...my first home, the beautiful meadow, my sister Kelyn, my birth mother's warmth and the last view I had of her while leaving the driveway of our house. I hope that she knew I loved her. I still miss her even though I now have a loving family.

What I discovered was that I could now remember my birth mother in a loving way without feeling disloyal to the wonderful family who took me in and made me one of their own. I am capable of loving both, and this trip made that realization possible. I would be forever grateful for that gift of peace of mind.

Traveling across the country made my going back to my roots and facing those feelings of being taken away a worthwhile endeavor. I found a balance between the loss of what happened so long ago and the acceptance of an entirely new way of life that was so worth living. Family was everything to me...past and present. A canine could have both, and I was proof of that.

Tomorrow we would begin our journey home. My dad figured that if we left the resort early enough, we could get as far as some place in Arizona the first day and then as far as Albuquerque, New Mexico the next. That would give us a head start for the last leg of the return trip. We would pick up Brightie when we got closer to home, and I was anxious to tell her all about the trip. After all, I had seen places along the way that were just awesome. It was a trip of all trips, and this cross country canine was ready to share all of the adventures with his best friend. In spite of all of her idiosyncrasies, Brightie is my very best friend. After all, she tolerates me in spite of the numerous times I tried to fool her.

Little did I know that this trip of all trips was to turn into something not only unforeseen, but also an event that would be fixed in our minds and lives forever...

# PART III
# THE AFTERMATH

I'm not sure if it was the acrid smell of the deployed air bag that caused a choking sensation in my throat or the realization that the car wasn't spinning anymore that brought me back to my senses. My canvas crate was tilted on its side, and my body was at an awkward angle in the back seat area of Sparky 2. I thought at first that I had been upside down, but that wasn't the case. What I did see that frightened me more than what had occurred was the fact that I could see pavement from what used to be the floor of the car's back seat. What ever happened ripped parts of the underside of the car right from under us. *Right from under us? Us?* Where were my mom and dad?

The last thing I remembered was the screeching sound of something that bounced under the car, blew the tires and ripped the underside causing the car to shudder and swerve from the road. After that, silence shared the air with the smell of burning rubber and smoke. It was then that I noticed no movement from the front seat, and I started to see my life pass before my eyes...just before the darkness engulfed me. In what seemed like a lifetime of events flashing through my mind, I somehow came out of the darkness and realized that we had been in a terrible accident. Now, my only goal was to find my folks. All I could see was broken glass and a shell of a car that used to be my mom's Sparkler on Wheels.

All of a sudden, I heard my name, and it was my mom calling to me from outside the car. Both she and my dad were out there, pale from the shock of the ordeal but apparently unharmed from the accident. Relief surged through my body as they retrieved me from the back of what was once Sparky 2. Seeing the extent of damage to the car made me realize how lucky I was to have been in my canvas crate. That probably saved me from being a canine missile when the accident occurred. Messing with the folks earlier by trying to get into the front seat with them landed me in the crate in the first place. I'm not trying to justify the less than admirable reasons that resulted in my being crated before the accident; nevertheless, that bout of mischief probably saved my life.

As we stood on the shoulder of the highway, amidst the tumbleweed that scratched the pads of my paws, I could see a semi-trailer truck about a quarter of a mile ahead of us on the shoulder and a car, minus all four tires, behind us. Looking at the remains of Sparky 2, I knew that our Guardian Angels were part of the Highway Patrol watching over us. Their presence had to be the only reason we were standing on the shoulder of the road...unharmed.

Within a short period of time, the state police came to the scene to assist and survey the situation. Apparently, the semi-trailer truck had lost its driveshaft which, in turn, bounced along the highway and under our car. After ripping the underside and taking bites out of the tires, it continued on its mission of destruction and took out the tires of the car behind us. What a mess!

The state police officer came over to talk to my folks. Seeing me wearing both a head collar and a regular collar, he inquired as to whether or not I would bite. While I hate to digress momentarily from the traffic situation, I feel it is necessary to address this misconception regarding my head collar. The strap surrounding my nose is not a muzzle that prohibits biting...nor is it a rubber band as was once asked of my mom while in a shopping mall. The head collar functions like a halter on a horse and is a method for easy guidance and control of a dog. I was not muzzled and didn't want that perception to be left unchallenged. I'm a lover...not a biter!

The state police officer was satisfied with my non-biting status and took all sorts of insurance information while my dad arranged for towing and a possible place for us to stay for the night. What were we going to do? Mom and I just stood on the shoulder of the road as the sun set slowly behind us. As darkness approached, the wind picked up in intensity, causing us to shiver.

At first, a regular tow truck came to the scene, but our car was so totally damaged that a flatbed tow truck was needed. Another hour passed, and the driver of the flatbed tow truck arrived with his very young son in the front seat. I thought that a bit strange, but who was I to judge the situation? We were in the middle of who knows where with no usable car and no apparent way to continue our travels.

The state police officer informed us that we were about twenty miles outside of Albuquerque, New Mexico. At least we knew where we were. To be precise, my dad did want to get this far in our travels today...just not in this condition. Under other circumstances, it might have been one of those glass half full or half empty observations. This was not one of them.

It was getting late, and we had been out on the shoulder of the highway for about three hours. It was really cold and windy as the sun set. This unexpected situation would never appear in any travel brochure regarding a cross country trip.

As the flatbed tow truck jockeyed into position to load Sparky 2, the police officer was trying to figure out how to get us all off the highway. He came up with the idea of my riding in the back of what was left of Sparky 2 while it was on the flatbed tow truck. Needless to say, my mom was strongly opposed that idea. There were just too many of us and not enough seats to go around. We still didn't know what we were going to do or where we were going to stay much less how we'd get there.

Just when there doesn't seem to be light at the end of the tunnel, something positive happens. Since the tow truck driver had his son with him for the day, his former wife was meeting him on the highway to pick up the child. I didn't understand that, but I didn't look a gift horse in the mouth either. My dad asked the tow truck driver's wife if she would take us to a motel in Albuquerque. He would ride in the tow truck to the car dealership and then to the motel with our luggage. Dad offered to pay her for driving us, but she wouldn't even consider taking money.

Through the kindness of a stranger, we were taken to the nearest motel along the interstate in Albuquerque. It took about twenty minutes to get there, and we were most grateful for the ride. Dad arrived about an hour later in the passenger side of a flatbed tow truck. Under other circumstances, it might have been laughable. Today, it was not.

After settling in to our one room accommodation, it was time for the folks to evaluate the situation. What was

275

important was that we were all safe and had survived a most incredible accident...unharmed. That was all that mattered. Everything else that followed was just an inconvenience.

We were now in Albuquerque, New Mexico without a car and had to make some sort of arrangements in order to get home. It sounded so easy, but nothing is easy when circumstances are unexpected. The car could not be repaired for at least a week, and rentals weren't available for three days. As a result, we spent those three days in the motel. To pass the time and alleviate some of the stress of the situation, the folks took turns taking me for walks. I was happy to help since there wasn't much for me to do, but I was doing double time on walks while the folks got things under control. Paw pads only handled so much wear and tear, but it was the only way I could help.

My dad was wonderful throughout this crisis. He took control on the highway after the accident as well as with the travel arrangements that followed. He made provisions for Sparky 2 to be fixed and shipped back home while we used a rental to get back to where we belonged. We belonged at home and the sooner the better. Dad did everything for us and most importantly, he made us feel safe.

Three days later, we left the motel for the trip home. While I like to think of us as a loving family, we had just about enough of the closeness in that one room. In addition to that, the pads of my paws couldn't take much more walking. Fortunately, there was no harmonica playing either. It seemed that every cloud had a silver lining. Sorry, Mom.

That day, we made it to a desolate place somewhere just before the Texas border. I have to say that the stars sure shined brighter in the darkness of the Texas sky. They were the brightest stars I had ever seen and looked like diamonds embedded in black velvet. In contrast, the motel left a lot to be desired. It was in the middle of nowhere, but my dad had driven all day and was very tired. We were lucky to even find a place to stay at this late time of night, so there was no quibbling about the accommodations.

We were put in the dog friendly section. Let me just say that it wasn't all that dog friendly since the dog next door yapped from the time we got there until the time we left around five a.m. the next morning. That yapping machine was clearly incentive to get an early start. This trip was becoming a saga of events that would remain in our minds for a very long time. Brightie was going to get a real kick out of this excursion.

We got as far as St. Louis the next day and spent the night in a motel under the shadow of the incredible Gateway Arch that illuminates the city. Fortunately, no yapping machines were spending the night on either side of our room. We hit the road very early in the morning in order to get a head start on the last leg of the trip home. We were all anxious to get to our destination, to pick up Brightie and to be in our own home again.

As we finally reached our home town area, we stopped to pick up Brightie. She was so excited to see all of us. She and I jumped all over each other and disregarded all forms of etiquette regarding proper greetings. We needed to say special "hellos" to each other and were determined to make the best of the moment. She was so excited to hear about our trip but questioned our change in vehicles. I told her that I would explain everything later but that I wanted to hear all about her fantastic vacation. There was no need to give her the terrible details of our trip home before she had time to share her thrilling experiences.

When we got home, I told her about our terrible accident as well as my belief that our Guardian Angels were watching over us on the highway. While hearing the details of the accident really frightened her, Brightie seemed to find comfort in my belief regarding the Guardian Angels taking care of us. It gave me great comfort as well, since walking away from that accident, unharmed, was nothing short of a miracle. We were definitely taken care of on that stretch of highway. There is no doubt about it.

Once at home, we settled into a routine…although nothing seemed the same. In the aftermath of the accident, we all had some sort of residual uneasiness. We were all so grateful for our safety, but each of us relived the accident in our own way for many days, weeks and months to come.

Sparky 2 was fixed and delivered by a flatbed truck the week after we got home. Even though it was restored and checked at the dealership, my mom didn't feel the same about her Sparkler on Wheels. She wasn't as comfortable in it as she was before the accident. Consequently, the folks traded it in for a newer model station wagon. The Sparky name and color were retired in recognition of the car's safety record. It only seemed right to do that. The replacement vehicle was dubbed the Blue Baron due to its deep, sapphire color and tycoon-like name. Unfortunately, my mom never felt the same about this new car. Sparky 2 had been her special car and always would have that position in her automotive hierarchy. This new car was just a vehicle to get from one place to another. Sorry, Blue Baron. Sparky 2 Ruled!

Dad carried on as usual, but I do believe in the quiet of the evening when all was safe and secure, he thought about the accident and how lucky we all were. He helped us through a most difficult situation and took charge when we were stranded on that patch of highway just outside of Albuquerque, New Mexico. He only thought of us and our safety. He handled everything during those terrible days following the accident as well. I had no way to express my gratitude to him other than to stay by his side and give some sort of comfort to him by my closeness. I wasn't usually very demonstrative, so my hanging around him was a bit of a surprise. I think he knew what I was doing. Dads are smart regarding things like that.

On the other paw, I had some difficulties with the time after the accident. Somehow between the time of accident and the realization that I had survived, my imagination had tricked me into thinking that I had relived my life. It was such a strange sensation, but it all seemed so very real to me. Seeing myself in flashes of events growing from puppyhood to adulthood was so very eerie. I wasn't sure what was real and what wasn't. What I did know was that all of those flashes of events shaped my existence and that perhaps, by reliving them, I might have a better understanding and appreciation for my life.

I spent a lot of time in my corner safety zone and relived those flashes of events in the silence of my thoughts...trying to understand why it all happened the way it did. I'll never know what was behind it all…only that it happened. As a result, I had a better perception of my life. I know it all sounds so profound especially coming from a dog, but actually surviving a life threatening event would serve as a wakeup call for anybody…including a dog. I can attest to that.

Months passed, and Brightie and I resumed our lives in a most productive way. We ate, slept, played in the yard, walked outside, went for car rides, jaw sparred and air snapped every chance we got. Intense thoughts of the accident faded in my mind, but there was always a faint echo of it present each day. I wanted to remember just enough to make me appreciate everything I have in my life but not so much as to make me frightened of facing the day. After all, I am a cross country canine who has seen the events of his life flash by and lived to tell about it. I do have quite the imagination, and it was definitely in overdrive.

Winter was closing in on us as evidenced by the gusty winds and the cold temperatures. Snow was falling steadily. Once again, the yard was transformed into a winter wonderland. Brightie and I weren't ready for the snow filled dog run and the blustery winds that pelted our faces. However, the season did have special meaning for both of us…in spite of the extreme weather conditions.

It was special because each of us came to our new family and to this home at the same time of the year. Our first experience with the winter winds and snow that covered the area, as far as the eye could see, shocked our California systems. We were so confused and frightened when we first arrived at this new home in what looked like a snow-filled land.

We also remembered how Marnie came to live with us around the same time of the year although she didn't come from California. She came from Michigan and had some experience with cold weather but not much since she was just a little tyke when she arrived. Marnie's enjoyment of the wintery season surprised us since it just made us shiver.

*Snow Puppy.*

Her attempts at deck diving into the pool of snow in the dog run made us laugh. Our dad went out in the middle of the night to clear a spot for her, and she just ignored his efforts by diving into the deepest part. That was our Marnie.

She was also responsible for the controlled chaos during the seasonal, holiday photo. The quest for the perfect photo was, by nature, fraught with tension. Marnie took the experience to a new level. Getting the perfect pose of the three of us was quite a monumental task...getting it while we were wearing some form of holiday garb or bell laden collars was another story. Nothing was sacred in terms of our behavior during this ordeal. Just as the perfect image was about to be digitally recorded, Marnie would reach over and grab my collar; and I, in turn, would grab Brightie's. The resulting rolling around the floor was typically followed by running around the room. Once under control again and in position, Marnie might roll over on top of me, and Brightie would jump on her. The digital acrobatics continued, and chaos reigned. It would become a "Tradition of Turmoil" with us, and Marnie started it. However, all it took was a stern look from our mom to end the frivolity. We quickly assumed our positions and were etched into the digital history of the holiday season.

*Mission accomplished.*

Brightie and I still carry on the "Tradition of Turmoil" in Marnie's honor. After all, it is a part of her legacy.

Aside from our fooling around, the season was one of remembering and reminding each other about the blessings we shared in our home. Brightie, Marnie and I shared so many experiences in this home of ours, and each one was special to us. It's where we began a new way of life, and each of us shared the same path in the beginning but chose a different road in the end. It is funny how things worked out that way. We are so grateful for everything. Even though Marnie wasn't sharing the season with us this year, she left her paw prints on our hearts, and we will always remember her for the joy and mischief she added to our lives. Now, she's sharing joy with someone who needs her, and that's

284

how it should be…hopefully without too much of the element of mischief.

The weeks passed, and winter raged on with bitter, cold weather, mountains of snow and icy streets. We didn't do too much other than look out the windows at the kids playing or sledding in the streets. Our excessive sleep time may have seemed like a period of hibernation to the onlooker, but it suited us just fine.

There seemed to be a bit of activity going on around us in the house, but we were so complacent that we didn't even bother to investigate. Had we done that, we may not have been so surprised by the gates positioned at various locations in the house. The puppy kennel, that each of us shared from generation to generation, was once again located in the kitchen area, and the toy box was positioned under the bay window. Seeing the small, elevated stand with the set of food and water bowls was the clincher. The red warning lights were flashing in my head at top speed. How could I have missed all of this activity? I thought sleeping was healthy, and yet the enormous amount of sleep I was getting shielded me from the folk's preparation of another possible Dooms Day encounter.

If Auntie Deb and Auntie Brenda showed up and the folks went for a car ride to pick up another package, we were

285

doomed to another year of mentoring madness. A short time after saying the words, the Aunties drove up in their car. It was already happening, and nothing would stop the ensuing chaos. It was now confirmed. Another puppy was on its way to our house, and the sorority house was possibly pledging another member.

Brightie was all excited about the prospects of a new puppy in the house, and why shouldn't she be? She never had a chunk taken out of her face by a puppy's razor sharp teeth. As a puppy, she was the chewer, and I was the chewed. I did not want that to happen again anytime soon. Brightie reassured me of safekeeping, and how ridiculous was that? She was determined to watch my back if the opportunity for chewing occurred. Was I going to allow this Get Me-Gimme Girl Diva to protect me? Remembering the pain of those needle sharp teeth embedded in my muzzle when Brightie was a pup was more than enough to say, "Bring it on, Brightie. You're hired and it's payback time!"

I was taught not to bite a lady and if this pup turns out to be a female and like Brightie was when she was a pup, I'd be in the same predicament. I'd let Brightie be my bodyguard in this situation. Marnie had been an easy and well-mannered pup. The odds weren't in my favor for getting another one like her.

While Brightie and I weren't qualified as assistance dogs, we were now going to be in a service capacity so to speak. Teaching a new pup the proper standards of canine behavior was a job in itself; and because of that, the Socialization Squad was established. We named ourselves as co-captains, and we were looking forward to our first deployment to the front lines with the arrival of this newcomer. Our special paw shake gave official status to the Socialization Squad, and we were ready for whatever was to come.

*Let's shake on it.*

To be honest, I wasn't as willing as Brightie was to go to the front lines, but I had already planned escape routes if necessary. Situational awareness was an attribute to the squad's success.

Our responsibility was to give this pup the necessary skills to get along with other dogs, to play nicely and respect the pack order in the household. It didn't sound like much, but it would take the entire year if done correctly. Brightie was just too excited about the prospect of taking charge of a newcomer. I'll be right behind her with an escape plan.

Well the "sniffing game" was played that night, but not with the same enthusiasm as in the past. I was worried about the newcomer and how our lives would change significantly when the folks returned with the pup. I went to my corner safety net and took some time to reflect upon all of the wonderful people and dogs who had been a part of my life. In my mind, this was the quiet time before the storm, and I needed to use it wisely.

I have such fond memories of my birth mother, her warmth and kind eyes. She cared for all of us and yet had to let us go to places unknown to live our lives. My mind centered on my sister Kelyn, who lives in North Carolina and how lucky I was to reconnect with her through my mom's friends, Auntie Jan and Uncle Don. Kelyn was just as silly as ever, and she could still catch a bug in midair. What a talented gal!

Then, there was Linus. While I referred to him as Mr. Pompous when he stayed at our house during my puppy days, he taught me how to be a gentleman in the canine world, and he did it with finesse and style. There will never be another dog like Linus.

Marnie was a pup to be cherished. She was gentle, kind and caring towards others. We were best buds and even though Marnie left us for service, she will always be with us in one way or another.

*Friends Forever.*

My Auntie Deb and Auntie Brenda took care of me when my folks were out of town and taught me how to play the "sniffing game." Launching myself onto the bed at night was a bonus.

They also took great care of Brightie when she became my adopted sister. However, she already knew how to launch herself onto the bed!

Thoughts of Brightie filled my head. She turned my world upside down with her Diva-like personality, razor sharp teeth and occasional pushy ways. But, she's just like that wart I talked about earlier in this story. She grew on me, and I'd miss her if she were gone.

*Thank you for being my big brother.*

There were a lot of other people in my life and events that shaped my future, but I would be terribly remiss if I forgot to mention my folks. They did everything for me and went the extra mile just to make sure that I had every opportunity for success in the world. I owe them everything and will attempt to repay them in some small way...every day.

This leads me to the responsibility of the Socialization Squad. Brightie and I will do our parts in terms of mentoring this newcomer. Although having Brightie teach this new pup to play bow, spin around twice and bark isn't all that promising. I'll be there, behind her in the safety zone, to keep the spinning and the barking to a minimum. That's my promise to the folks and to the new puppy. Other than that, we'll just teach the puppy to be the best pup ever.

I'm glad I had this time to think about all of the people and dogs who have influenced my life. It helped me to prepare myself for the upcoming task, and that starting bell was about to ring.

We heard the car pull into the driveway, and both Brightie and I rushed to the appointed greeting position. We were both trembling with anticipation. My tremors might have been a bit out of fear of the unknown, but I wouldn't advertise that. Brightie was taking this Socialization Squad very seriously and assumed the most perfect greeting position. Mine was a bit sloppy, but that only allowed for a quick retreat if necessary.

Our folks were taking so much time in the garage that we could hardly stand the excitement. As the door slowly opened, I thought about the awesome challenge that awaited us on the other side of that door and hoped that we lived up to the expectations.

Then we saw her in our mom's arms. Another sorority sister was here...only this time we got a blonde one. She was so blonde that she was almost white in color. She had lots of wrinkles and had the blackest nose I had ever seen. That nose would have a tough time turning pink on that little darling. She looked mighty cute, but I knew better than to be misled by cuteness.

While the world might be a stage for others, our house was now the stage for this newcomer, and all the props were in place for the show. The multi-generational, puppy kennel was in position, the gates were up, the set of bowls in the elevated stand were located near the kennel and the toy box was positioned under the bay window. Everything was ready for the newcomer's arrival; the guest of honor, the star of the show, was now entering the house.

As Brightie and I exchanged knowing glances, I knew that this opportunity offered great potential for fun and excitement. This production would run for at least a year, and the Socialization Squad was ready to rock and roll on this particular stage. As the curtains rose for the opening of this new show, what resounded in our heads were the glorious words that caused our hackles to tingle and hearts to flutter with excitement.

For us, it was now... SHOWTIME!

# The Story Teller

My name is Kessen, and I live happily with my mom, dad and best friend Brightie. Telling this story has been an adventure for me and I hope for you as well. I continue to enjoy mentoring puppies as part of my responsibilities in the Socialization Squad and consider preparing puppies for possible assistance to be a most serious assignment.

In my free time, I enjoy fooling around with Brightie, taking long walks in the neighborhood, playing in the backyard water bowl, going for car rides and eating special treats. Based upon the events and adventures in my life, dreams really do come true.

*Thank you for sharing my journey.*

# About the Author

Jennifer Rae Trojan, who writes as Jennifer Rae, lives with her husband Chuck and her two dogs, Kessen and Brightie in a western suburb of Chicago, Illinois. Since retirement as high school guidance counselors, Jennifer and her husband have worked with various service organizations as puppy sitters, puppy raisers and volunteers with animal assisted therapy. They both consider being a part of a potential assistance dog's journey an adventure, a privilege and a true labor of love.

Kessen and Brightie, who serve as co-captains of the Socialization Squad, enjoy the mentoring involved in working with new puppies. However, they are mostly in it for the excitement, the fun and above all, the treats.

The family looks forward to their next puppy...

# Acknowledgements

Fostering a puppy for possible assistance, training a therapy dog, rescuing a shelter dog or raising a well behaved pet are not easy tasks. They are joint efforts among owners, families, friends, relatives, trainers and even strangers who lend a helping hand throughout these endeavors.

While I thank all of those people who have helped with training and socialization, there are certain individuals who need special recognition in terms of their assistance:

First and foremost, I must thank my wonderful husband Chuck for his endless support, enthusiasm and willingness to help me with this endeavor. He not only assisted with the dogs, but with so much of the housework that I avoided while writing this story. Without his love, encouragement and endless proof reading, this story would not have been written.

Debra Steller and Brenda Whitesell, the Aunties, have been the best of friends and have also loved and cared for each of the dogs. I can't thank them enough for their kindness to me and to them. Entrusting the dogs to anybody else but their Aunties is not an option.

Jan Jaeger, who raised Kessen's sister Kelyn, has been a true friend throughout this sibling adventure. She has been one of my major sources of laughter from across the miles. In addition to that, her expertise as a Certified Trainer has been and will continue to be a major resource for training tips in the years to come. Many, many thanks.

Carol DeMaio has been a good friend for well over forty years as well as my brainstorming buddy throughout this writing experience. Her insights and constructive criticisms provided invaluable assistance toward the completion of this story. While I appreciate her efforts and expertise, her friendship is the greatest gift.

Alice and Jerry Meyer welcomed each of the dogs to their home while the pups were in training. They truly appreciate and acknowledge the tremendous job of an assistance dog. I am forever grateful for their friendship.

Julia Havey gave of her time, guidance and use of her dogs for socialization purposes. Allowing Linus to spend time with each of the dogs was a gift not only to them but to me as well.

Pam and Rick Osbourne, who offered encouragement, assistance and publication know-how, advanced this story from an idea in my mind to its final publication. Their efforts have taken me one notch lower on my Bucket List.

Kathleen Deist, dubbed the Goddess of Grammar and Punctuation, contributed her time, efforts and expertise toward the successful progression of this manuscript. I'm fortunate to have her as a good friend as well as a qualified consultant.

Lisa Kruss, of petphotos.com, graciously granted permission for use of the photos on the covers of this book. Her generosity is greatly appreciated.

When I tempted fate with the changing of my computer settings, Mary Krystinak brought my manuscript from confusion to clarity through her computer wizardry. I am so very grateful for her help.

Special thanks to the service organizations across the country that provide the puppies for fostering. Giving individuals the opportunity to share in a puppy's journey toward assistance is such an incredible experience. It's one that lingers in the hearts and minds forever.

Kessen's actions, struggles and antics have blessed this family with love and laughter on a daily basis. Without his shenanigans for inspiration, this story would not have been written. His allowing me the use of his name as my main character is greatly appreciated.

Finally, to the dogs of the assistance world, I sincerely thank you for the work that you do for others. On any given day, most of us can't even imagine how much you do to help those in need. This story is just as much yours as it is Kessen's.

CPSIA information can be obtained at www.ICGtesting.com
Printed in the USA
LVOW11s1802171014

409268LV00002B/4/P